Mamba

Ma

by Stuart Cloete

Houghton Mifflin Company, Boston

The Riverside Press, Cambridge, 1 9 5 6

Books by Stuart Cloete

NOVELS OF SOUTH AFRICA

Watch for the Dawn · The Turning Wheels
The Hill of Doves · Congo Song
The Curve and the Tusk · Mamba

NON-FICTION

Yesterday Is Dead · Against These Three
The Third Way · The African Giant

POETRY

The Young Men and the Old

The Riverside Press
Cambridge · Massachusetts
Printed in the U.S.A.

Dedicated to Man's dream
of the fair unknown woman

Chair de la femme, argile
idéale, O merveille

. . . .

Et qu'on ne peut, à l'heure
où les sens sont en feu
Etreindre la Beauté
sans croire embrasser Dieu?
VICTOR HUGO

— Can one indeed, when the senses are on fire,
Hold beauty without embracing God? —

Author's Note

This is the story of the struggle of a man against the forces of evil which drive him, and those of good which inspire him; of a God-woman concept; of a search for truth and beauty, in the confusion of today, where there is no precedent.

In a world in which a man like Einstein wished he had been a plumber and a boy may consider himself lucky to be born a cripple; in which men fear to reproduce themselves, so great is the danger and insecurity in which we live.

Reality has been lost in a maze of gadgets, beauty has been replaced by glamour, music by the radio, and life itself by the films. We work without pleasure in order to eat, and having eaten, try to escape through the door of entertainment into a dream, from which we wake still more dissatisfied. We have forgotten that we are still part of nature, as much a part as a sparrow or a fish, as much as a geranium in a pot or a field of oats. Now only in Woman and through her, and the act of love, do we become part of reality again. This alone is unchanged and unchangeable but, hoping for too much, this also fails and only anaesthesia remains.

Orthodox religion has failed us, science has betrayed us. The old are without wisdom, the young frustrated by the complexities of existence. Man, having destroyed the wild beasts of the world, has attacked its green skin on which he lives like a parasite on the back of an ox, and now in his fury is turning inward upon himself. Yet, despite it all God still exists, and beauty, and woman, and love.

Who is this *I* who writes? How many have there been, changing from year to year, from hour to hour, minute to minute? Wanting this, getting it and then wanting it no more. The *I* that was mad with love, with passion. The *I* satiated. The *I* furious. The *I* asleep. The *I* hunting intent on death, the *I* regretting death when I had killed, love when I had loved. The *I* that stroked a dog. The *I* that kicked it. In each mood, in every phase, the *I* was different, so that what I said in one mood was not what I should say or even think, in another. Was this *I*, this concept of my personality no more than a figment of my own imagination? Were none of us real individuals? Were we merely composites, amalgams as it were, of various characteristics, which blended into a whole so variable that nothing could be guaranteed of anybody; everything depending on health or sickness, day or night, on the amount of alcohol that had been drunk, on the whether we had just made love or were about to, on how solvent we were at any given time, or the weather? Was it fine or wet? hot or cold? on how we were dressed? For a man's mood changes with his clothes as much as a woman's.

I see all this clearly now. The *I* that I have been. The *he* and *she*, the *him* and *her* of those that I have known have been multifaceted, multishaped, like the animals that revolve around the fixed stage of the carousel, the merry-go-round of my childhood. All one can be certain about when one gets to know an individual is that the zebra, the spotted horse or the ostrich that we originally met will reappear if we wait long enough.

What we know of others, what we call their characters, is no more than a catalogue of their animal characteristics. Some men are all lion, some all jackal. But most of us are a mixture of crowing cock, braying ass and ostrich, with our heads hidden in the sands of ignorance and prejudice.

Looking back I have some difficulty in seeing myself as I was then, when I stood five feet eleven and weighed a hundred and seventy pounds. My hair was dark brown, my eyes hazel. I was fit and hard, fighting fit as they say, riding three hundred miles or more a month. Sometimes of course I went down with fever. But I seem to remember myself as very alive — strung on the wires of my aliveness. Now my hair is grey, distinguished-looking, I believe it is sometimes called, my back stooped, my waistline much bigger. I am well preserved as they say. Very well preserved, if I consider what my life has been. Pickled inside with the gin of a million martinis, varnished outside with the lacquer of a million social encounters, tired with the cynicism of events that seem to repeat themselves day after day, week after week, month after month. But then in that strange long ago everything was new. I found a photograph of myself the other day, taken in Leopoldville. It has faded badly, been eaten a little by termites and fish moths. In a way I have suffered the same fate. My eyes have faded in color, my contours, even the contours of my personality, are blurred like those of the picture. I was, I suppose, a fine young man then — *un beau garçon* — but then we were all beautiful and strong in our youth, or if we weren't we think we were. This might be a definition of age — a slow imperceptible fading; imperceptible till we find a portrait of ourselves as we were then. When we say: Was I really like that? Is that really me?

Is this a story of deterioration, or something that might happen to any of us were we similarly exposed — or is it simply another alibi?

Contents

Mamba

1 The Room

After it happened I stayed in the Congo for several months. This seemed the safest and wisest thing to do under the circumstances. Then I went home to England. I took with me *The Forest*, my first book. It was taken by Collins. It was taken in America. The films bought it. My farming days were over. I went to the United States and remained there. My life is too well known to bother with any recapitulation of either my failures or my successes. Anyone curious enough can find the bones of my career in *Who's Who*. For the meat they must go to the daily press. The blood I reserve. The nerves and sinews I am tearing out now. That is my present occupation. They quiver like landed fish and take as long to die. I was once a fisherman, so I can observe the similarity. They lose color, as anything alive must do as it dies. The eyes become opaque. Glazed.

Death can first be seen in the eyes of a dying man or beast. Often I have seen death in the eyes of a sick ox or cow or horse or dog when I was farming. In the eyes of young men dying in battle who know their end has come, a look of resignation that goes beyond despair. I have seen it in the eyes of animals I have killed for sport or meat. The mirror is filmed with death. It shows in the coat, too, as in the scales of a fish. For there is living color in the coat of an animal, a bloom — an iridescence. The topi and the blesbuck shine like bronze. They have purple and blue lights in the sunshine. Sometimes when I see a patch of iridescent oil in the gutter of the city I think of them in the sunshine. I think of a mole I once caught as a boy. It shone with all the color of the prism, of the rainbow — till I killed it. I wanted its skin. I pegged it out and salted and dressed it. But I never did anything with it. Its beauty had gone.

The eyes of a beast or a man about to die are blank. They are already looking into the next world. Like someone going on a journey. They have projected themselves beyond the present into the future. You see it in the eyes of old men too. The tired eyes of men who have seen enough.

Nerves and sinews are the wires, the cords, that articulate the human puppet. I once saw a chimpanzee pull the fingers off a man's hand. But the sinews remained unbroken, stretched like the strings of a harp between the ape and the man. My sinews are stretched now, bared for examination.

It is difficult to explain what I feel when I see a beautiful woman. My heart leaps in my body, climbs into my throat.

Tears are near to my eyes. There is a sinking pain, as of sickness or hunger in my belly, my loins. I do not have to know her. Only to see her crossing a street, passing through the lobby of a hotel, sitting on a seat in a park. But most of all walking, the way pretty women walk, balanced on the pinpoint heels of their sexuality. Aware, but with downcast eyes, and a rebuke on their lips for the emotion they have deliberately aroused. Do all men feel this? I feel the same looking out to sea from a high cliff, a feeling of beauty, of danger, of pain low in my belly. The same looking at a butterfly poised upon a flower. Some beauty can be touched, be held, almost possessed. And each time we hope to reduce the size of the *almost*. Reduce its length. It is like a book that we have not been allowed to finish. That has been taken away. We feel we have missed the best of it. We wonder what the end would have been and say: Now we shall never know. So with a woman. We continue to turn the pages of her personality. We seek her body under her clothes with our hands, with our eyes, with our lips. Then we seek her heart, her soul, her mind. But we never reach the end of her. There is no mystery in woman. There is nothing to solve. What she holds is life itself, as the vehicle through which it must pass. She is the cup of God. Beauty, all beauty, is felt in the genitals. A man is castrated by his awful sense of beauty. That is the pain he feels low down in his belly. That is his fear. He knows that beauty is the knife that will emasculate him, cut his strength away with its awful power. That is why so many men avoid all beauty. They say beauty is for women. Art, music, sculpture, books, flowers for women, because women cannot be emasculated.

In America, by slow degrees, my life became something of a scandal. I went to the dogs and, to turn it into a poor joke, most of them were female. But of all the women the last, Gloria, was the worst and the most beautiful. The most abominable, without virtue, without honor. She was lascivious and cruel, a woman who could only be placated by gifts of furs and jewels. These were her twin passions. A woman with the nature of a cat, and an aquamarine set about with diamonds for a heart. But never was there a woman with a sweeter smile, a softer voice, or a body more graceful, pliant and yielding. She was like a peeled wand, a flower swaying in a soft spring breeze. I wonder why I write about her. Perhaps I hope she will read this. Perhaps I hope to create some mild disturbance in that icy heart. To move it. For that calm organ has never beaten one jot faster with my love while I lived and how often have I watched it pulse in her naked bosom.

She has been like a drug. I see now that that is how I took her. A habit-forming woman whose use had to be constantly increased. Gloria, my desire, my lust, the woman who, epitomizing every grace of her sex, disgraced them all. Resisting nothing, permitting everything, giving nothing but her beautiful soulless shell. Utterly irrelevant to life, but the essential core round which I revolved for years, the axle of my squirrel cage, the open vein that has bled my life away. So it is to you, Gloria, that I tell the story of my love for Helen. You have asked me about her often enough. It was the only thing I kept from you. My one secret — now you will have that too.

In those African days I was unknown to more than thirty or forty people. I did not write. But I was, in my small way, and for a short time, happy. Writing, according to some psychiatrists, Freud among them, can be classed as an escape mechanism. In disaster some escape into illness, others into crime, still others, those with a hitherto unsuspected talent, into the arts. I must be one of the latter because, only after it was all over, did I begin. Till then I had had no idea that I could write seriously. Looking back, I see that my aim was to create a tolerable world, to create people, characters whom I could control, and escape, as Freud says, in their company from the unbearable reality.

Unreality since then has become my dwelling place, unreality in all things, so that even Gloria was like a bad dream, something to be lived through. I think I always knew that one day I would come out on the other side as if time were a river. It was like being in a dream and knowing that one is dreaming. You say: This is a dream; soon I shall wake up.

Now like a surgeon I am cutting through the flesh of my life. Like a butcher I have smashed the bone, cracked it for the dripping marrow. Like a strong-handed washer-woman I will wring out my life like linen, till the last drops drip from between my fingers. Having dared to go so deep, to take this step, I am free at last. Not happy — that is too much to expect — but free for a few days, just to look around and see the world again. It is as if I had been underwater for years, seeing everything — except Gloria — vaguely green.

It is difficult to say exactly when my plan took shape. Certainly meeting Anna on Fifth Avenue had something to do with it. Anna grown up, settled and happy-looking. She knew me at once. I could not possibly have recognized this woman whom I had last seen as a child of eleven in

Africa. But she had been following my career in the papers. There had been pictures sometimes, when a new book came out, or a new divorce, or I sold a picture.

She seemed glad to see me. She asked me to lunch with her. At Schrafft's, of all places. It was years since I had been to a Schrafft's. The Plaza, the old Ritz, the Waldorf, the Colony, 21 or the Stork Club were more my line. But she was meeting her husband. I must meet him. That was why she would not lunch with me at one of my places. I think I wanted her to know that I was well known and respected, even if it was only by head waiters. There was so much to say. Yes, she had three children. Two in school and one baby. She had called him after me. I didn't mind, did I?

It all came back as she talked in her explosive, happy, disconnected way. She had not changed — she'd only grown.

We met William. Not Bill, William. A shy young man of about her own age. A professor at some obscure college in the Middle West. I don't remember which now. A nice boy with a crew haircut. Archaeology was his line. He'd done some excavating in Egypt.

What did I think of Zimbabwe? Did I know it? I did, and I told him.

"I'd like to work there if we could all go. It's a good climate, isn't it?"

I said, "Yes, it's quite healthy."

Anna's brown eyes shone with love, with excitement.

"You're happy, you two?" I said.

"Sure we're happy. But we're five."

They irritated me. Like a damn platoon, I thought.

Five of them. Too much had come back too suddenly. I asked about her father.

"Colley?" I said.

"Father died last year," she said.

I said I was sorry. She said, "He was glad to go. He was in pain and he was not afraid. He wanted to see mother again. He said it had been too long, and I could take care of myself now. At least William could."

I asked them to dine but they couldn't. It was their last day. I can't say I was sorry. It was hard to believe that I had loved her so much as a child.

But that must have been the beginning. Anna had brought the Congo back, and the Congo meant Helen. They were too happy. I was consumed with jealousy at their happiness. I knew so few happy people. None in fact. And people, what a lot of them I knew. Hundreds, all friends so none of them were friends. Damn it, I didn't even know the last name of some of them. We were that intimate. But what a way they lived. How we all lived, each keeping a kind of ledger account. Checking drink against drink, party against party. And if it was a woman — love against gifts. They never took money of course. Only things — like fur coats, trips to Florida or Europe, a new coupé, some trifle like a diamond and platinum clip. That was how they differed from whores. And they drank more.

Then I saw Helen on the corner of 48th and Park. I followed her, almost running, but she disappeared into a big apartment house. No one would tell me who she was. The elevator man said there'd been no such person. I described her — a fair girl in a grey suit, small grey hat, mink scarf, grey suede shoes. She loved suede. Carrying a grey snakeskin pocketbook. No such person. I forced my way into the manager's office. It is important, I said. Most urgent. They got the doorman and threw me out. Talked of calling the cops.

I saw her again on Madison and was nearly killed by a bus as I tried to follow her. When the bus had passed she had gone. I drank more, which means a lot. I was certain she had risen from the grave. That this was a new miracle. I knew of course that she was dead. After all, I had buried her. I had lain her down in the bottom of the grave when Henry had passed her body to me. I knew that she would have changed as much as Anna had, that she'd be over forty now, not at all like the blond girl in grey whom I had seen. I knew all this, but believed none of it. I was two men. The one who had seen a passing woman — a pretty stranger, and the man who had seen his love — young, beautiful as ever. I knew that this was a young woman who just happened to look like Helen. But I knew, too, that she was Helen, even if she did not know it. That Helen's spirit had passed into her. That if I could hold her in my arms she would be Helen. That all my troubles would be over. I would rest, and sleep again. That I could take off my armor at last and hang it, like a coat, in her room.

How few men can ever take off their armor with a woman and be themselves, naked and defenseless. You dare not. Even with it on you feel them prying at it, feeling for the chinks with long-nailed, painted fingers. Trying to get under your armor, under your skin. To get you helpless, a victim of their every whim. Today men no longer have long hair so it's their armor the Delilahs are after. The defenses that they have built up, the scar tissue of a thousand hurts. If they only knew how freely men would take off their armor if they were not afraid. That sometimes this is a man's only dream. To be natural, to be himself, if only for an hour. And this is where the whores, the real ones who take money for it, cash in. With them a man can be himself. They know the name he calls himself is false. That John is really Ben, that Frank is Peter, but they don't care and the men don't care. They only know that here, in some walk-up apartment, they are who they are — themselves — something they can never be with the women they have married.

When a man thinks like this he is mad. I am mad because I think like this. I am off the beam. Round the bend in a fourth-dimensional world. But with it I am excessively sane. I have made plans. I have found a new garage. Not a garage really, but a kind of open shed where some delivery trucks are parked. There is no night watchman and I have been given keys to the big gates and the postern. Two Yale keys to freedom. In the building which forms one of the walls of this yard there is a generator that runs continuously, day and night, the way machines can and men can't. A machine will do just what it is designed to do. I do not know what I am for. We do not even know what a baby is for. Certainly not as a toy for some mentally arrested girl. You see what I mean? The way my mind keeps going off the rails. But I'm cunning. I'm full of tricks.

The room I have taken at the Wagram on West 45th Street is on the fourteenth floor. It has a splendid view of the city. I can see the McGraw-Hill Building close by and the Empire State pinnacle reaching into the sky. Below me is a sheer vertiginous drop without offsets, a temptation to anyone with suicide in his mind. But what a selfish, thoughtless way to end things. A mess that someone would have to clear up. When I was a child my mother had always said, "You've got to learn that there is not always going to be someone to clear up after you. Put all those things away." But how could a man who jumped put himself away? I had learned my lesson. Then there was the psychological effect on the passers-by, on the pedestrians who saw a man burst like a grape on the sidewalk before their eyes. It might have serious and far-reaching effects on their nervous systems. But the ordinary suicide is a very selfish, and usually stupid, person, who kills himself on impulse or for revenge.

However, I have no doubt that the Wagram, which is a very efficient hotel, has means of coping with suicides mashed on the sidewalk. They seem to have thought of everything. There are even, so I was informed by a leering bellhop, call girls on the premises. Not ordinary girls, mark you, though presumably made like them, but chorines and small-time actresses who work this racket on the side for special customers. Men like myself, he seemed to imply. And he'd be glad to introduce me. I gave my budding pimp a dollar bill. He said, "Thank you, Mac. Thank you. Anytime you want."

So I looked like that, did I? Then I consoled myself by thinking that perhaps he tried it on everyone.

The room has everything a room should have. Bed, bedside table with a phone and phone book, a big bureau, a small sofa, an enormous closet, a pincushion with threaded

black and white needles stuck in it. There is a stand for
my suitcase. There is a good bathroom. The water runs
hot as soon as I turn it on. It has everything a man requires for not dying in. It is a room in which it would be
equally impossible to live. No one has ever lived here.
People have simply passed through it like water running
through a sink. Commercial travelers, ordinary travelers,
men just passing the night waiting to catch a train or a
plane or a boat; women alone, waiting to go somewhere,
waiting for their lovers. Women who had left their husbands. Women who had neither husband nor lover. The
room carried the impress of a thousand personalities, their
fingerprints were on everything. A thousand hands had
opened every drawer. But their soul-prints canceled each
other out. Their hates, loves, fears. Their desperation and
their optimism. For nothing had been static here. Everyone had been occupied. Preoccupied with business, with
love. I wondered how many lovers had lain entwined on
the bed. How many women had sobbed themselves to
sleep. How many men had passed out on it, dreaming
their drunken dreams of orgy. It was all here, but ex-
punged, expurgated by the room's impersonality, its sterility,
its hygiene.

How different from my apartment on East 63rd Street
that I had left last week, saying I would be away for a
fortnight. There everything spoke of me, was intensely
personal. Everything had been bought by me, chosen by
me. Except for the presents that I had been given. Very
charming and expensive things, some of them. I was always interested to see what financial risks people would
take when they wanted favors done for them. The beauti-

ful lures with which they would disguise the hook of their desire. Or was I being cynical, unjust? Was a *quid pro quo* always expected? Was there no impulse, no generosity, no altruism?

When did people become like that? When did the boy turn into the man, the girl into the woman, the puppy into the dog? Suddenly, the tail ceased to wag. Suddenly, they wanted more than love. But there were some people who didn't. Suckers. Suckers like Anna, like Helen. Suckers who were happy. Perhaps only the suckers were really happy. That was quite a thought.

I looked round the room again, fixing it in my mind for no reason except that I wanted to. It was a detective of a room, unrecognizable in a crowd of rooms the way a dick is supposed to be in a crowd of people. Change his hat and you'll never know you've seen him before. Change the draperies, the bedcover, and the room is lost. It was like the room in the story by Poe about the girl and her mother in Paris. What was its name? Was it by Poe?

I wondered if anyone ever remembered this room. Room 1404. The women who had been made love to in it, or the men who had loved them? But then lovers do not see rooms, feel beds, or even need them. But this is the room in which I will finish my work. I am almost at the end of it now. For the first time, I do not care if it does well. I do not care whether Hollywood buys it or not. It is a great relief. Leaving my beautiful apartment has been a great relief too. Sometimes a man becomes overburdened with his possessions. Even with his memories. For these are possessions too. Possessions that nothing but death can take from him. And, like a dog coming out of the water, the time comes when a man must shake himself free. Free of everything, even of his life, for life is also a possession. No one can take life away except God or the Government, or the man himself. The knife or bullet of the assassin is an Act of God, like a hurricane. No one knows this better than I.

How interesting it all is. This complete lack of responsibility, of worry. How easy once your mind is clear. It was lack of clarity which had made me drink, lack of it that had driven me from the arms of one woman to those of another. How soft and fragrant they had all been. How moist their lips, how useless to my purpose. A man cannot drown himself in a teacup. He cannot satisfy himself with a cocktail when he has drunk from the sea.

It was wonderful to be able to think the truth. I had always known that in civilized society one could not tell it, but only now, in this new mood, did I realize that one never allowed oneself even to think it. A pretty thing, the truth. Like a flower growing out of the bulb of reality. Like a lily.

Today I had been to the Bronx Zoo to look at my friends the hyenas. There was a truth for you. After that time I never poisoned another. After all, it might be Henry. And I couldn't kill him twice. Besides he had been a soldier. Soldiers should be shot, not poisoned. I was quite pleased with myself, thinking of my sensitivity. I had remained a gentleman. There were still things I could not do.

There was nothing in the room of my own but my clothes, toilet articles, suitcase and a couple of cushions. They had looked a little out of place at home too. Dark red velvet with a border, and tassels of gold cord. A little vulgar, but very comfortable. But then the woman who had given them to me had been a little vulgar too. Taste was almost the only thing she had not got. I felt myself smiling.

When I am ready, I shall make an end. Very neatly, in my cream-colored Cadillac. I have the section of hose already in the closet. I have tried it on the exhaust for fit. I am a very neat and tidy man. I would not like any mistake to mar the final drama. Or is that a delusion on my part? Shall we call it a joke? For the beginning was a joke too. That was what made it so terrible. I had believed at the time that he had caught us out and was making her pay. But perhaps it was just another of his goddam practical jokes that happened to end fatally for his beautiful wife. Or was it? You see I knew Fatty Seaman. Full of jokes he was, but each one, like a scorpion, had a sting in its tail.

This will be, in a way, a confession of murder. In another way, the story of justice being dealt out to a man who was bad in every way. But since I was his wife's lover my evidence may be open to suspicion. I do not think I did right in becoming her lover, but I am not the first man to have an affair with a married woman, and I shall not be the last. There were feelings of guilt and sin on both our parts, and both of us paid the price. She with the terrible death her husband inflicted on her, and I with her loss, and the weight of justice upon my soul. How many judges would condemn a man to death if they personally had to hang him? In mitigation I can only say that when a man of thirty falls in love it is very often with another man's wife. Besides, it was in Africa where proximity is dangerous, especially if the woman is lovely beyond words and her husband, to take a phrase out of detective fiction, "a beast in human form" — a sadist. Of course, being known as a writer of fiction, this posthumous story may be regarded as fiction. Psychiatrists may even call it a wish-fulfillment story. They may say: That's what he would have liked to have done. In his unconscious he made love to this woman and killed her husband. Very well, let us have it that way — fiction. A story in the first person.

I do not consider myself a bad man in the accepted sense. There had not, until after this incident, been more than five or six women in my life, and they had been incidental. Nameless. Featureless. Just bodies to whom I had been driven and which, satiated, emptied of lust, I had left and forgotten. In fact, as a young man, I did not really care for women. I was afraid of them. I avoided Helen to begin with. I fought against her. But time I could not fight against, neither of us could, and time caught us, and thrust us into opportunity. We sank into it afraid, as if it were a morass — a bog — and once caught, it held us fast. We could not get away. Feeling ourselves sinking, we could only cling more fiercely to each other. After that, as everyone knows, there were more women. Gloria was merely the last one, the best known.

And now, my friends, what will you make of the story? Because I am leaving you, I can call you my friends. How odd — for years you have been reading my stuff, have kept me, but then I would never have dared to call you friends. Yet you are, collectively, the best I have ever had. No one else has been so kind.

Is it fiction? Is it a confession? And if it is, how could I be dangerously involved after so many years, without witnesses and in a strange country? And in that case, why must I end things? Indeed, shall I? At the moment I am not sure. But if I do I dedicate both my story and my death to Gloria — the fulfillment of all men's desire. The devil's greatest achievement. For if a good woman is the final work of God, a wicked and beautiful woman can be the final work of Satan — the perfumed pitchfork with which he hustles the better class of sinners into the fire-box of hell. You see, friends, the better class of man does not fall through theft or murder. (Did I say murder? But in my mind it was justice.) He does not cheat or lie. He may drink but that is only stupid, so it's women that the devil uses. Women and gambling. But women most of all. So when you listen to Gloria singing next, just look at her and her manifold perfections. Undress her in your mind. Why not? She will not care. Not if you have the money. Imagine her flesh in your hands, her warm, perfumed body. Warm — it's more than warm, it's hot — as if she always ran a temperature. That, I think, was one of the many things that held me to her for so long. Helen's body had been hot too. And soft. Oh, she is the dream of all fair women. Watch her on the dance floor, watch her do her act — her song and dance routine — and then forget me, friends, forget and applaud.

I have thought much about this search for beauty, for the perfection that I hoped to find in woman after woman. A search which it is possible to equate with a search for God, for the ultimate, for truth. Can one, I still wonder, hold beauty in one's arms without embracing God? But I see now that for this to be fully appreciated the individual must first be destroyed, must become, as it were, one with reality. No longer himself but part of a much greater whole, an infinitesimal drop in the vast ocean of all living things. What I sought was the ultimate experience, ecstasy. I sought what is looked for by celibate monks who fast and pray, and flagellate themselves, to destroy themselves, and thus achieve the same end that I sought and almost achieved by other, opposite means.

This seems to be the great paradox, that perhaps the aim of the libertine poet and the celibate monk are one. That both are sexual, for to deny sex is to acknowledge its power, to be in its thrall. Sex then, by its exploitation or negation, is the only means of approaching the fullness of life; the only way to come near to birth, to death, to God himself, is through woman by the positive or negative poles of mystery, of creative force.

These are strange thoughts that come to me. I wonder, too, if there is not some common ground where in after life the murderer and the suicide meet with the murdered. A kind of spiritual Potter's Field where those who take their own lives or another's may find their victims, and explain their acts. A place where I shall meet not only Henry Seaman and Helen, but myself, as a separate entity, the *ego* I have spent my life serving, but of whom I know so little. The *I* that has driven me, possessed me, ridden me as a man rides a breakneck horse.

Of course there is no Gloria. But there have been several. There is someone now, but not Gloria. Gloria is the name of failure, of love given and lost. Of all the women whose hearts I have not touched. There have been Helens too, or near-Helens, women who returned my love, whom I have exploited as the others exploited me. But perhaps they were all one woman. That it depends on the man, that disillusion produces disillusion. Perhaps the contempt I had for those who loved me was repaid by the contempt of their sisters whom I loved. I have pursued beauty as a kitten pursues its tail. Chased rainbows looking for the pot of gold. I think Helen had been a Gloria before I met her, that some of my Glorias have been Helens to other men. There is no pot of gold. There is only the search for it which perhaps I have taken more seriously than other men, seeking God in Beauty, and failing to understand that He is everywhere. Would I have loved Helen if I had not seen myself reflected in her eyes? Was that all I wanted, a reflection of myself?

Perhaps there is glory in degradation, and degradation in glory. Perhaps the first really will be last and the last be first. Perhaps the search is greater than the reward, or is its own reward. The shadow greater than the substance. That God is the search, the power that drives a man to seek, that living is God, and God living — the living God. That this is all He permits while we are still alive, and death the ultimate truth. The end of life its real beginning. It will be interesting to find out.

Perhaps I can say to God: I have lived hard, fought hard, sought hard. Is this enough?

2 The White Men

There are certain difficulties in telling my story. It must be told in the first person; by *me*, the *I* of the narrative. The hero and the victim of a series of events whose beginnings go back to my school days and whose ends are not yet, not even with my death, for there are no ends. Events in which I (or anyone else) was concerned must continue — by the concatenations of circumstances, by emotional chain reactions — to exert pressures, just as ripples continue to circle over a pool long after the stone that caused them has sunk.

I tell the story in the first person because that is what I know, what I experienced. But I must also tell something of the other participants of this curious drama. Now their stories I do not know. I deduce them. I put some words into their mouths that I never heard, that possibly they never spoke, but which, from their acts, must at least have passed through their minds as thoughts. And since this is a final effort, since the dead have no shame, I need disguise no motives, neither my own nor those of my friends, enemies, or lovers. Usually we give too much credit to our friends and too little to those who dislike us. We do this because they are often more right, in their estimate of our characters, than our friends. We hate the truth. So we must hate those who tell it. It is necessary for survival to hate the truth, to destroy one's benefactors, and betray those who love us before the burden of their love becomes too great to be borne. What we require of our fellows is admiration, envy, and subservience. A man even kicks a dog that loves him too much. It requires too much of him in return. Love must be returned or destroyed. Sadism may be an escape from love. But how unfortunate for the sadist that he must always choose a masochist as his victim. And that the act that should have driven him away, binds him ever tighter to his master. That is a great bond. The bond of slave and master, for the master can no more get free than the slave. The bond of hatred is a great bond, as great as the bond of love, or greater. I have known both. An old love is more easily replaced than an old hatred, and missed much less. I have been amazed at the power of the spleen in the human organism. Odd that it should be more powerful than the heart.

And a man's will — what a strange thing that is! He may train it, like a gun, sight it on a distant point, pull the lanyard, fire the charge and then cease to be a free agent any more. He has bound himself like a slave to the master of his idea. He must proceed like a projectile down the trajectory of the years.

All this one learns when it is too late. For this is the wisdom of the devil that God has kept from man and only the wicked know. God has kept the wickedness of man's own heart from him. This is His great mercy. This is the bitter fruit of the tree of knowledge that God has forbidden and which the devil tries to thrust into every hand. And here we are tricked again, for the form of the fruit is not that of a fruit. There is no apple, no orange. Oh no, the fruit can be in the bottom of a bottle, in the soft warmth of a woman's body, in the pips of a playing card, the satin sheen of a horse's neck. It can be in the smoothness of a gun stock, or in the coolness of a dagger blade. All these are fruits and many more beside.

This is the story of some of the fruits I have plucked and of how sometimes I myself have been plucked as fruit. For in evil there is a kind of marriage, a giving and taking, a sacrament as it were, where the participants merge and are indistinguishable. In the struggle it is somtimes difficult to distinguish the assassin from his victim or the lion from his kill. And then naturally, to set sin off, there must be some good, some light in the picture, for without it there would be no form or substance.

Above all this is a story of love, or what passes for love, and its opposite, hatred, or what passes for hatred. Both great emotions which first send a man mad and then destroy him.

Nothing is new. There are no new pictures or stories. There are only new arrangements, new combinations, new presentations. Every thumbprint looks much the same as every other, but each thumbprint, like each life, is individual and different.

The animals are different too.

The leopard does not eat on the ground disputing its kill with the scavengers. It kills from a tree, leaping onto its prey — a young wildebeest or an impala — drinks its blood while it still lives and then carries it into a high fork, where it may leave it for several days, coming to eat at dusk or in the grey light of early morning. The cheetah courses its buck like a greyhound, chasing it, catching it, turning it as a greyhound turns a hare, and killing it on the turn. Elephants dig for water with their feet, their tusks and trunks. And under the water the river horses gallop gracefully, leaping all obstructions. They are often accompanied by fish which keep their skins clean of vermin. On the surface the graceful lily-pad runner — slim brown birds with white throats and bellies — pull parasites from their nostrils, eyelids and ears. In the hot sun the lions lie like great cats on their backs with their feet in the air. So much of my life has been spent with the animals. With their infinite diversity and mystery.

None are identical. And sometimes I wonder where it stops. With ants and earthworms? With maggots? How odd that something created by God should find pus so beautiful and seek it for a home. That the fly should use it as a cradle for its white oval eggs. How much odder that medicine now has returned to the use of maggots in the cleansing of wounds and to discover that God created maggots for this purpose.

I do not think there will be maggots in heaven, but there may be dogs and cats, and horses and singing birds. And trees, and perfumed shrubs and vines. If there is a heaven it is pleasant to conceive it as a garden filled with living things — like Eden before the fall.

This is in a sense a testament. And these documents, in spite of their being wrapped up in legal terminology, are often remarkable for the truths they tell. It is by his testament that a man's true loves and hates are known. The big legacy to the mistress whose existence his wife never suspected, sums to children born out of wedlock. The proverbial shilling to the son who thought he had hoodwinked his father. A will can be a very humorous document, and lawyers must get a laugh out of some of them. A twisted kind of lawyer's laugh.

Since I must choose a point to start, the story might as well begin with a night in Africa. It has not ended yet.

Henry said, "What will you have, Colley? Whiskey, gin, beer, Cinzano, Dubonnet. We've got the works, haven't we Jim?"

"Yes," I said. "The works." And we had too. Drinking had become a kind of hobby with us. Though I did not like it much, it was something to do.

"Tonic and lime juice," Colley said. "The usual . . . "

"Can't tempt you, can I?" Henry said. That was another thing we had a lot of. Temptation. Temptation and boredom. Maybe they went together. Sometimes I wondered which came first, like the chicken or the egg. But Henry had got Colley tight once. It had been very dark on the stoep and he'd given him a whiskey — sometimes he did take a very weak one — with angostura bitters in it that disguised its strength. He hadn't known the trick. This was typical of Henry. He never knew when to stop.

I was against fooling about with Colley. It was like being unkind to a child. He was a good man. One of the few I've ever met. A missionary, and as a rule I don't like missionaries. Mealymouthed, psalm-singing lot of bastards who put Mother Hubbards on the Africans, teach them hymns and then talk about their converts. Converts — hell! But Colley — the Reverend John Franklin Collison — wasn't like that. He practiced what he preached, which made him a difficult neighbor sometimes. And then there was his little girl Anna, a sweet kid. Like a bloody little angel.

I looked at him sitting there in his old khaki. A skinny little man with a head too big for him. It was shaped like a gourd, big on the top and tapering down to a thin yellow face covered with little knobs that made it hard for him to shave properly. A dried-up little man who looked very queer sitting beside Henry, who was so fat. Fatter now than he had ever been.

Nobody said anything. There was nothing much to say. We'd said everything we had to say months ago. I wondered sometimes why we met as we did. And then decided that there was some kind of attraction, a current that drew white men together in Africa like twigs in a whirlpool. That was what we were — white twigs in a black flood. We had nothing in common but our whiteness and the vestigial memories of our homes, our youth, our mothers, at whose knees we'd learned to pray and not to do the things we did now. There was some masochism in it, and regret, and memories, and a kind of braggadocio that made us like to conjure up the past in order to insult it.

We figured that we were the salt of the earth. Kings in a way. Masters who shouted "Boy!" and boys came. Who said "Come here!" and they came. And "Go there!" and they went. We killed things. Wild animals. And ate them.

We called it sport but we had to kill them if we wanted to eat meat. (I'd given up shooting before I came to the Congo, except for birds, but I'd hunted a lot once.) We took our lives in our hands and pretended we liked it. Maybe we did like it. Sometimes it's hard to remember. Danger is good when it's over. Like pain, you don't remember it. And when it was over we felt good.

For man and beast danger is part of life in Africa. There is not a buck or zebra that does not have to run for its life at least once each day. All the time those great liquid eyes are searching for enemies, those great flickering ears listening, those moist black nostrils snuffing. People who know nothing say isn't it wonderful that wild animals are always so well. That they have no sickness, are never ill. They do not realize that an injured foot or something that in a man would be no more than a cold or a headache, means death to an animal. The margin of safety is so slight.

We were strong and brave. Colonials. *Colons* as they called us here in the Congo. The cannon fodder of Western Occidental culture. Patrols thrust from civilization to feel out the enemy in the forest. Guinea pigs for the study of tropical medicine. Purveyors of curios to the children of our relatives at home.

Henry Seaman — Fatty as we had called him at school — was a gross pink and white man with very fine, very fair, almost white hair. He looked like a big, very powerful baby. At school he had been a bully but very few people had known it. Only the few he bullied in secret, and they were afraid to tell. Besides he was so nice to them in public, buying them ice cream and cocoa and jellies in the grubber, that no one would have believed them if they had talked

about it. In those days he was not so much fat as cur-
vacious, rotund and rather angelic-looking.

Fenshaw, the art master, undressed him mentally, stuck
little wings on him, and shoved him up onto the ceiling
with a bow in his hand and a little quiver on his back.
A cupid, and a nasty one at that, was Fenshaw's opinion.
But in the Common Room no one thought much of his
opinion. He was an artist. He not only taught art but
painted pictures and sold them. One could have no confidence in a chap like that. I met him years later and he
told me what he'd thought. Besides, Fatty Seaman was a
good slow bowler, a splendid swimmer and in the shooting eight. He worked hard and always did well at exams.
So taking it all round he was popular at school except for
Fenshaw and some of the smaller boys. Most people thought
him very funny. He had a quick wit and a passion for practical jokes. He was a good mixer, with a remarkable talent
for knowing on which side his bread was buttered.

He regarded himself as a good fellow. A comical chap
who was always up to something. A "life of the party" boy
who later on had quite a way with the ladies. Because,
by then, he had acquired that other fat man's talent: he
had become a remarkable dancer. He floated round the
floor like a great chunk of thistledown spinning in the
breeze. Charm oozed out of him like sweat, and with his
sweat. But the beads of perspiration on his pink brow were
in no way offensive. They looked as if they belonged there,
like dew on some big pink and golden flower.

Everyone was fond of old Seaman, of Fat Boy, or Pinky
Seaman. He drank pink gins in those days, but it had to
be Plymouth. As I say, everyone liked him except some

of the people he had played his jokes on. But they were either men much smaller than he, or girls who were alone. The kind of girls one meets in bars and clubs, who are called tarts at one end of the social scale, and hostesses at the other.

One of his favorite and funniest tricks was to drop a white mouse down the front of a girl's dress. Oh, that was very funny, especially if she became hysterical. He bought the mice for this purpose at Gamages. He'd carry them in a little carton with string handles. He'd hold one up, white and struggling, making little swimming motions with its tiny pink feet as he held it by the tail, and then, neat as a whistle, down it would go between some girl's breasts. The mouse nearly always got killed, mashed on the floor under someone's foot or struck down by the barman's broom. But it was worth it. It really was. Women were so silly.

No one ever knocked him down. A lot of men wanted to but he looked very big standing there balanced on the balls of his feet, rocking lightly back and forth, his hands half open hanging loosely at his side, his friendly, bright blue eyes challenging anyone who had no sense of humor.

A quirk, that's what it was. Old Fatty was all right really. Okay. No harm in him, but a bit of a bore when he'd had one or two and started being funny. Everybody liked old Seaman, or said they did. Nobody loved him. Some of them said he was a fairy, some of them said that he was woman mad. None of them really knew anything about him. He had his haunts — some small clubs and bars, some restaurants. If he wasn't in one you might find him in another. If he wasn't at the Sherry Bar he might be at the

Bunch of Grapes. If he wasn't there it might be worth trying the Antelope or the Café Royal. The word spiv was not current in those days but that was what he would have been called today. He had no known means of support but he lived well. He belonged to no regular club, only to those small, rather doubtful, artistic drinking establishments where a little gambling generally went on in a private room and there were bedrooms upstairs.

I had forgotten most of this when I met him again at The Old Metropole in Johannesburg. But it came back by degrees. I had been out of a job then and he'd offered me one. So perhaps I had not wanted to remember.

He was the last man in the world whom I would ever have thought of as a farmer. But he was, and a good one. His father had farmed in a big way in Yorkshire. After the war, where he'd done very well — active service had suited him — Fatty refused to go back and had lived on his gratuity and his wits till the money was done and he'd let his wits run away with him. He'd been just a bit too clever a couple of times and decided that Africa was the place to go. England had temporarily become too hot to hold him. I still didn't like him but had learned to live with him.

We sipped our drinks. They were warm. We had no ice in those days. We lit cigarettes and threw them away. They drew badly. Henry lit a new one.

A boy brought out a hissing pressure lamp.

"Take that bloody thing away," Henry shouted. "My God, do you want every bloody insect in the Congo on the stoep?"

The boy took the lamp away.

Colley said, "I want to talk to you about something."

"Talk away," Henry said. It was not one of his good days.

"One of my girls has been raped," Colley said.

"Well, I didn't do it," Henry said.

"One of your boys may have though."

"Which one?" Henry asked.

"She won't say."

"Well, what do you want me to do? And how do you know it's one of mine?"

"I don't know. But it's not a mission boy," Colley said, "and I don't think it's anyone from the village."

"That's what she says," Henry said. "Rape," he said. "If he'd paid her it wouldn't have been rape."

"It's worse than that," Colley said. "She's got marks on her."

"What sort of marks?"

"Scratches. Deep ones. She thinks he was going to kill her."

Henry threw his cigarette away. "What are you trying to say?"

"I've seen them before," Colley said.

"Seen what?"

"Those marks. When I was in West Africa."

"Well?"

"She told me where it happened. I went there. There was some spoor on the ground."

"Of course there was spoor . . ."

"But it wasn't all man's spoor. There was a leopard's with it. Tomorrow I'm going to the Chef de District. I want to leave Anna with you. I'll be away three days."

"I still don't see. . ." Henry said.

"Of course we'll take her," I said. He'd left her with us before. A sweet kid.

"Leopard men," Colley said. "Aniotos. I've been afraid of it for some time. Now I'm sure."

"My God," Henry said. "I thought that was all over."

"Nothing is ever over in Africa," Colley said. He was silent for a moment, and then he burst out: "How I hate the forest. Any evil can live in its darkness."

"But there are leopards about," Henry said. "A couple of people have been killed in the last year or so."

"Yes," Colley said. "Women, and no body found till it was rotten, putrid, hardly identifiable. Why weren't they found? Or were they found and not reported? I can feel it," he said. "In the village. In the mission. There is fear," he said. "There is silence. Even the tam-tams sound different." He looked up. "Have you lost many calves lately?"

"No," Henry said. "Not for six months, and I trapped that one."

"Curious, isn't it?" Colley said. "If there are leopards about? No calves, no dogs in the village. No goats. Only women. Do you remember when they were killed, Henry?"

"Not exactly. A year or so ago."

"Exactly," Colley said. "Before the rains."

"What is all this leopard-man business?" I asked. I had heard of it but that was about all.

"It's a secret society. They kill for various motives but the strongest is for medicine. The witch doctors want parts of the human body. The genitals, the skin of the face, the heart, the lungs. The leopard men get them. They dress up in leopard skins. They use wooden pads on their feet to imitate the spoor. They kill with iron hooks that make scratches resembling those made by a leopard's claws. But there's a difference. When a leopard strikes, at the end of the stroke its claws contract and the scratches get narrower. When they are made by a leopardman they don't. Her's didn't," he said.

"How did she get away?" I asked.

"Something frightened him," he said, "and she was greased."

We didn't say anything. Colley sat with his elbows on the table, his hand over his eyes. I knew what was biting him. One of his girls going half naked and greased to meet her lover in the forest.

It was quite dark now. The night falls suddenly here, like a black cloak punctured by the bullet holes of the stars. The savage brilliance of the day is smothered by the more terrible blackness of the night in which death walks. Of course it does not look like that. It looks beautiful, indigo, star-spangled, the great Milky Way reversed, spread like tinsel. The silhouettes of the tall trees and palms are as romantic as anyone could wish. From the distance comes the throb of the tam-tams, the never-ending pulse of the African night. Fireflies flit and hover. Later the moon would rise blood-red, illuminating the edge of the forest like a flame. Come up, rising visibly as you watched it, like a great orange cheese. The man in the moon here is a rabbit sitting back, reclining against its outer curve as if it was a chair. The Br'er Rabbit of our childhood's tales came from Africa, brought from this moon to America, by the fables of the slaves. This was the moon of sacrifice; of madness that raced men's blood, like tides, into a fury of desire, of nostalgia, of love, of memory. It worked like strong drink. Whatever a man felt was intensified by its pale light. Restraint was lost. If a man hated in the full of the moon he killed. If he loved, in the full of it, he took his love willingly or otherwise.

It even affected me, with my blood thinned by fever, my ears ringing with the bells of quinine. It struck some atavistic chord. For hundreds of thousands of years our ancestors had danced by the moon's blue light, as the Africans danced today. In the light of the moon the savage and the civilized man meet on common ground.

Everywhere round us people were waiting in the darkness for the moon, the sister of the sun, to rise. The silence was profound. The sound of the drums did nothing to disturb the massive stillness of the dark. They only made it more apparent, as the clothes of a woman may emphasize the beauty of her nakedness.

We were surrounded by mystery, by the inexplicable, in which we white men were irrelevant, separated from such reality by the steel and concrete of our culture, distant though it was. Understanding nothing, we hovered on the periphery of the unchanging forest and hated everything, striving to overcome our fears with our alcoholic contempt.

This was not a new mood, but Colley's story had pointed it up. His presence had. Here was a man of God facing the terrible gods of field and forest and river. Setting up his Cross against the fetishes. Pitting his two-thousand-year-old crucified Christ against the bloody sacrifice that was still warm. His tin tabernacle against the great ju-ju trees, the silk cottons, big-buttressed, rooted in the fecundity of Africa.

I do not know what the others felt. Colley, I was sure,

was thinking along my lines, but he had his faith to sustain him. I had no faith, only the knowledge that such faith existed. I should like to have had it. It was impossible not to believe in God here.. But much harder to think of Him as merciful. I had seen so little of mercy in Africa. Only cruelty and savagery, against which, as a defense, one developed one's own savagery — a core of hardness that had to be worn like a breastplate. But how heavy it was. How hard to live for days alone, with only guns and the contents of the medicine chest to defend one's physical life, with only alcohol to support the spirit.

Henry got up. I heard the sparklets syphon squirting. He was having another drink. That was one of the answers. Have another drink. And another. Courage and hope came out of a bottle. So did despair.

Behind us, behind the living room on the back baraza, Marie-Thérèse would be moving around on her bare feet. If anyone was about she kept out of the way. Big-eyed as a buck, almost as invisible when she wanted to be, she was part of the background of the ranch. Part of the white man's background in Africa. One of the warm, female shadows that sucked out his blood, and with it, his life and his integrity. Smooth, sleek as a leech, she cast her dark aura over the establishment. I heard the gramophone playing softly and knew she was squatting over it. Her silk-wrapped head slightly cocked over the revolving disk, a stable lantern on the floor beside her.

But who was I to judge? Henry had been here much longer than I. Perhaps she was part of the price that he had had to pay for his knowledge of Africa and the African. The price of knowledge might be such intimacies. Once

I would have been shocked. Then surprised. Now I felt nothing except perhaps an occasional twinge of jealousy. Men did not cease to be men because they went into the wilds. And women remained women. These women were all women. There were no other aspects. They were all women as a horse is all horse. They knew what men wanted and had known from their naked childhood. A man only wanted one thing. I thought of the white women who said that, women who knew nothing. These women knew nothing in words, they only knew the invitation of their bold dark eyes, of their satin skins and writhing hips.

One day it might happen to me. I saw no protection from it. There is an emptiness in a man without a woman. A vacuum in his life, and these women knew it. They felt it. They knew the exact moment when no more could be borne and then they were there. It was as if a man wanted a flower for his buttonhole and suddenly one sprang up beneath his feet. They struck as a snake strikes but there was no serum against them. This was the ancient temptation of a man's loins, the living thing, the one member beyond his control. Priests had fasted, had flagellated themselves, had immured themselves, had emasculated themselves in this endless war against Priapus, but only a priest could resist forever the bodies of such women, if they passed continually before him. Women who brushed their hips against him. Who stood with their breasts tip-tilted before him, inviting him, laughing at him. Women who knew. Women who thought he was mad to resist.

These were the night thoughts. The moon was up now — a golden ball riding the sky. The silence was broken with its light. The tam-tams louder, more compelling, the fireflies paler, their brightness stolen by the moon. There were the cries of occasional beasts in the forest. The killers, or the killed. Bursts of sweet perfume came from the frangipanis. The garden was illuminated. The plains looked like silver paper. Beyond them was the forest, ink-black, that divided them from the sky.

"You'll stay to dinner?" Henry said.

"Thank you," Colley said.

"What about Anna?" I asked. I loved that child. "She'll be all right, I suppose?"

"Oh, yes," Colley said. "She expects me to stay. She said 'If they ask you, you'd better stay.' She'll just go to bed."

Henry called the boy and said: "Le père is staying to dinner." Colley was a Presbyterian but Henry always called him Father.

The boys brought the Tilley lamp into the sitting room and set it on its high stand. Then they took it down and pumped it up some more. I watched the light increase with the pressure through the fly-netted window. A big moth fluttered against the lamp glass. It threw a shadow as big as a bird against the whitewashed wall. A bat swooped past my face with a rustle of leather wings. The light came through the windows in a yellow patch. Except for the dim lanterns and fires of the natives there was scarcely another light for fifty miles. All over Central Africa there were these little bright pinpricks of white man's light. And how fragile they were, dependent on kerosene that came thousands of miles across the sea, on mantles that smashed if they were touched. But while they burned they burned brightly, and when they went out they were dead, as if they had never been. Was that what we white men were here? Lights that went out. And if we left would it be as if we had never been?

Then Colley said, "Would you do something for me?"

We both said, "Yes."

"I wonder!" he said.

"If we can help you . . . " Henry said.

Colley got up. "Would you pray?" he said.

Before we could answer he got down on the mud floor on his knees. We did the same but more slowly. It was years since we had prayed. It was most embarrassing. Colley said nothing aloud but I could see his lips moving. I muttered what I remembered of the Lord's Prayer.

After a few minutes Colley got up.

"Thank you," he said. "That was a fine thing to do." He put his hands on our shoulders as he stood between us, reaching up because he was much smaller than either of us. "I know how hard it was for you," he said. "But thank you. Thank you again. 'Where two or three are gathered together . . .'" he said. "Two or three. That's all we are, but we are a mighty host."

Poor Colley. He really believed it.

3 The Black Men

Next day things looked very different. It was hard to believe in human leopards, in Colley, in the fact that we had knelt like children on our own stoep in prayer; that the night had been filled with ghosts and menace; that a raped and tortured girl was being nursed back to health and sanity at the mission.

There was nothing sinister now in the patch of forest that crept, from its main impenetrable mass, out onto the open veld. Hard to believe that this brassy, burning world would ever be dark again; that night must fall, and the night thoughts come again. That was the curious thing about Africa, that each part of it was so separate from all the other parts. That the night bore no relation to the day. At home, in the weak dullness of the sunlight, evening seemed reasonable, and the evening so prolonged that night came as no surprise. Even the landscape in Africa had the same quality of separateness. The foreground was unrelated to the middle distance, and the far distance of the mountains seemed a thing utterly apart, as though each was divided from the other by some invisible gulf.

As divided as black men and white men were, living in the same world, with the same organs, the same blood, the same brains, but separated by an invisible psychic gulf, so that though they might stretch their hands out to each other their fingers never touched. A man might sleep with a black girl and be no nearer to her essential reality. This was more than the sexual difference, more than just a man and woman difference. Never here were the black and white, the male and female welded into a composite blend of man and woman, into a couple that formed a human whole.

One needed different values here. A new measuring stick. The Africans were animists. The trees, the rocks, the fields, the rivers and lakes were, to them, all personalities inhabited by spirits, possessed by gods; all to be feared and placated. Even such things as floods and droughts, as tempests and tornados, assumed human qualities. They were more than manifestations, phenomena — they were things, each with its own malevolent individuality.

We were in the throes of a drought. The world of grass and trees was being throttled by the strong hands of the sun. The sun was male. The sun was angry because he was alone. He wanted to mate with the storm and produce his offspring of crops. If Colley was right this might account for the leopard murders — for the sacrifices; for the death of a selected individual so that a community might live. If there was no rain there would be no crops — no manioc, no yams, no bananas. If there was no rain there would be famine. It was obviously better that one should die than many. And certainly no help could be expected from neighboring tribes.

Fortunately for us there was still plenty of grass, and though it was very dry it kept the stock alive. The river had not failed completely. There were deep pools left in its bed. So the cattle were all right.

This was what concerned us, but it was easy to see why the Africans were anxious. They were not cattle people and had little stock. I patted my horse's neck and kicked him into a canter. Peter was a good horse but sluggish, as horses often are when they have been inoculated against horse sickness. They live but are never quite the same. But we understood each other. He knew his work. And we had another bond. He was a South African too.

There was nothing much to do today. I was just riding round looking at the different herds. I would end up at the dip at the homestead and check its strength so as to have it ready for tomorrow. We dipped every five days and that kept the ticks down pretty well. The life history of some ticks is such that seven-day dipping does not kill them. They may fall off their host and continue their breeding cycle without ever coming into contact with the arsenic. Today I believe the dips are much improved. But today everything is much improved except the quality of life.

It was very pleasant cantering over the veld. It wasn't even terribly hot yet. I watched the sky for vultures. If anything was dead or sick they would be there, waiting for the end, sailing in wide circles or perched with hunched shoulders on the nearest trees. It was strange how colorless the day world was. How the brilliance of the sun bled out the blueness of the sky. It seemed to be bleached into a sickly paleness. The grass was yellowish white, the trees and bush a dull olive. The ground was iron hard, like red cement. The harsh herbage broke like twigs beneath the horse's hoofs. Here and there the nests of the termites rose like spired churches, like miniature red cathedrals out of the veld. These were live nests, inhabited. There were others, long abandoned but indestructible as concrete, out of which tall trees grew. Still others were topped with grass, which winter killed, lay flat like a man's hair over nests that had been rounded into heads, by time.

This was one of the great open spaces where men were free but it was curious how it oppressed one. With so much space one was reduced in size, in importance. One could understand the organization of the Africans into tribes, for only in organized masses could men resist this immensity. This was what drew white men together, too, into little conglomerations, where they coagulated like blood. That was another thing. One thought too much here. One was too much alone. One began to talk to oneself. But it was only serious when one began to answer oneself — to carry on conversations with oneself in two voices. I pulled up my horse. There was the herd I was looking for, with its herders, in a fold between the low rolling hills. There was not a cloud in the sky, not even the little ones that fleck it like bits of cotton wool and may eventually build up into rain. There was no sign of the drought breaking.

In the village under a big silk cotton tree the elders were grouped round the chief. Their spears were driven butt first into the ground beside them. They chewed kola nuts and tobacco and spat. They were waiting. But waiting meant nothing to them since they knew nothing of time. They were content. Sometimes they passed round a gourd of palm wine. They had been in the same circumcision group as boys. They had hunted and fought together as young men. They were closer than brothers. Men of one age, and one mind, of one experience.

No women or children were to be seen. They were in their huts or in the fields. They were afraid. Last night the fetish men had run through the village with their bull roarers and had beaten any women or children they found outside with long wands that were as thick as a man's finger.

A black and white short-legged goat wandered past them. An emaciated sow with dragging serrated teats, surrounded by her litter, dug hopelessly for roots. Some small chickens scratched up the dust or lay sunbathing with extended wings. Some pigeons cooed on their cote.

Everything was still, superficially normal, but there was a brooding atmosphere over the place, an invisible miasma.

An old man came towards the group. Three younger men followed him. Everyone knew he was coming. But no head was turned. He walked through the squatting elders with his young men behind him. He was a tall man but bent and withered with age, shrunken onto his ancient bones. Round his neck encircling it several times and hanging to his belly was a necklace of large odd-shaped colored beads and coral. On his head was the head of a python. The skin came over his shoulders, went round his waist and dragged like a train behind him. Below the snakeskin came a kilt of leopard and monkey tails mixed with strings of small dried tortoises, threaded one above the other and the skulls of animals — rats, cats, monkeys and birds. Round his ankles he wore iron rattles.

His guards were naked but for their loincloths and the white zebra strips of kaolin that marked their bodies. In their hands they carried whips made of great lizard tails barbed with leopard fangs.

The old man stopped in the center of the group beside the chief. He raised his hand. The elders raised their hands. A kind of deep sigh went through them. They moved on their haunches. The old man's will had passed over them like a wind over the corn, bending them, causing them to expel their breaths.

He said: "There is no rain."

They echoed: "No rain."

"There must be water," he said. "There must be moisture. Can the seed sprout in the dry ground? Can the nut increase, can the guinea corn shoot without moisture? Can a man's seed be planted in an arid womb?"

"There must be water," they said.

"There must be rain. The sacred soil must be moist as a woman's womb, where the man's seed can grow, ripen and burst forth like a fruit wrapped in its bloody pulp."

"Water," they said. "Water . . ."

"And blood," the old man said. "Without blood there can be no birth, for is not the soil the womb of the gods? Is not all increase one increase — that of the crops, and the beasts and the women? Can these mysteries be separated one from the other? Is not all fertility one fertility, all birth one birth, all increase one increase? Are there not seasons when the men must lie in the open fields with the women, when all men are one man, and all women one woman, and all increase one increase? A season when man's seed and blood must mix in the shadow of the sacred trees. A season when all women are wives to all men and all men husbands to all women, as the soil is mother to every grain and is fertilized by the rain that falls upon all equally, blessing them with its moisture. Who can gainsay this? We know it in our hearts as our fathers knew it." He paused. Then he said: "Before the white man came there was rain. The yams were as big as elephants, the women's bellies were fat, the manioc carrots were like a strong man's arms."

"That is so," they said. "Before the white man came . . ."

"Before he came," the old man said, "the gods were served with blood."

"With blood," came the chorus.

"Is cocks' blood blood?" he asked.

"It is not blood."

"Or the goats'? Or the bulls'? Are these blood?"

"They are not blood."

"There is only one blood that is acceptable to the gods," he said. "The blood of the goat without horns. The blood of a man or a woman or a child. This all men know. But it is now forbidden by the white man . . ."

"It is forbidden," they said.

He said: "But the forest is large. It is dark."

"It is dark and large."

"It is secret," he said.

"It is secret," they said.

"And we have the means. We have the leopards back among us. They have returned. Once again the gods have sent them to serve us in the ancient manner."

He drew himself up. He seemed to grow. He seemed to

become young again, lissom, his skin seemed to pale to yellow, dark spots appeared to come out on it, his eyes to turn green and blaze. He moved through the elders with his followers behind him. They, too, seemed to have changed. They did not walk as men out of the group, they slunk like leopards, silently on velvet pads, delicately, soundlessly, touching no one.

No one saw them go. One minute they were there, the next they were gone. In the dust there was the dragged spoor of a great snake.

In his little hospital Franklin Collison was talking to the girl. He had done everything he could for her but she was worse. In a few days she would be dead. She was afraid to live. But he wanted her story. He wanted to hear it again to check it. To be certain.

"You were going to meet a man?"

"Yes," she said.

"That is why you were dressed like that?" He meant in native costume and oiled with castor oil instead of the white mission blouse and skirt.

"Yes," she said.

"And you met him in the forest as arranged?"

"Yes."

"Then it was he who . . . ?"

"Yes."

He knew this was a lie. It was not her lover.

"And the leopard?"

"That was afterwards. It sprang upon me."

"It was a real leopard?"

"Oh yes, it was a real leopard."

"Then what you told me was not true?"

"No, it was a lie. I am sorry. Soon I shall die so I do not wish to lie anymore. I am a good Christian girl."

"You will not die."

"I shall die," she said. "There is no other way."

"Way of what?"

"Of ending this thing."

"Then there is a thing?"

"Oh no. There is no thing. It is only that I am afraid."

He knelt beside her bed. God help her. God help them all. He knew what had happened. She had gone out to meet a lover dressed only in a loincloth and pagne — a cloth like a tablecloth, wrapped around her. She had been freshly oiled with castor oil. That was how she had managed to escape when the leopard man had raped her. He had probably been frightened by her lover, who had heard her cries, and she had slipped out of his grasp. But now she would acknowledge none of it. She knew that if she did get well she would be killed by the leopard men, or by poison. This time there would be no mistake. In her mind the leopard men were leopards. Christian baptism had not destroyed her belief in lycanthropy.

So she would die because she would will herself to die. She knew there was no point in living because death would only be delayed. Those condemned must die and it was easier to die here in the mission hospital. To die peacefully instead of terribly. To die painlessly. Colley knew he could not save her. No one could save her. But if the leopard men were unappeased there would be a new victim. And what was the good of this story now? Where was the evidence? Who were the witnesses? The authorities would believe nothing. They would not want to believe. The Leopard Society is stamped out, they would say. It is finished. It belonged to the old days. Belonged with cannibalism and the rest of the things that had ended with white rule.

But he knew that these things did not end. He had worked in French West Africa as a young man. He had friends in Sierra Leone, he knew about the borfima fetish, about trial by ordeal, about the esere bean. What did he not know? He thought about those two young men at the ranch. He prayed for them. They were good boys. Too good for Africa. This was no place for hot young blood unless it had the support of religion. Their very strength, their boldness, would be their undoing. Strength in a man and beauty in a woman were sometimes the devil's weapons. As a young man he had been revolted by white men who had black housekeepers, as they called them. Now he was more charitable. It was a bad thing. But he was not sure that it was wicked. It was at least explicable — almost inevitable under certain conditions. Ordinary standards failed in Africa, or at least were not fully applicable. Henry's mistress was not the worst thing here. This was the worst thing. This spotted devil that had reared its head in their midst.

Anna Collison was neither a child nor a woman. Forced into precocious womanhood by the climate, she was held back from it by her environment where, without playmates other than the little Africans who trooped after her, she lived in a curious world of her own. A fairytale world of archetypes, of angels and witches, of black evil and white good, of animals, trees and flowers, of birds and insects, of her father — from whom all goodness flowed in a never-ending stream — of an ardent Christianity overlaid, without her knowledge, by the more beautiful of the native beliefs and myths. She was a kind of dark-haired Alice in this forest Wonderland.

Able, without flinching, to help her father dress wounds in his surgery, she still ran with the flying hair and the light feet of a child. Her greatest quality was that of wonder. It showed in her great brown, wide open eyes that held a continual air of surprise. Her mother, whom she resembled, she scarcely remembered. America, which she had left as a child, was a blur of bright lights and sky-scrapers, of noise and ice cream. The history her father taught her was hard to understand against this jungle background. America, her country, seemed very far away. Like heaven. Someplace to which she would go one day, as her mother had gone to heaven, but which, as the days passed, seemed to come no nearer. Within the limits imposed by Africa she was well educated, even academically advanced for her age. Her father taught her by means of a correspondence school in New York which specialized in such things, sending out papers, correcting them and returning them again. In this sense she attended school. But the Congo was much more real to her than the Hudson. Leopoldville more real than Boston.

So far nothing had marked or damaged her. She was intact, unsullied, like a piece of fine white china decorated with the deep gold of her innocence. This was her father's gift to her. The result of his education. For him there was no evil, only illness of the mind or body.

Anna's mind was a free, untrammeled thing that took

wild flights like those of a flushed bird. Only thus could she rationalize her academically acquired knowledge with the African tales she heard about her. Tales in which the trees were really possessed by the spirits of the dead, and animals talked like men; where there was no sharp line between dreaming and waking, or life and death. By changing things a little, by compressing one belief here and another there, she made her knowledge fit into the basket of her hopes. Her father might have been shocked at what she had made of some of his teachings, the Africans would certainly have been surprised at her interpretations of some of their beliefs. Peter and Paul were both robbed to create a composite design that suited her, however incredible it might have been to others.

Anna knew that one of the mission girls had been hurt. She knew nothing of rape or leopard men. At the moment her concern was with a big lily which had been out yesterday and was now dead. It had smelled so sweet. That she could not smell it again made her sad.

Henry was working on his stock books and accounts. In a week it would all be over. He was going on leave. Six months away from all this. From the cattle that he loved, from Marie-Thérèse with whom he lived. From the sun and the heat of the dry season, and the damp of the wet. He was excited. England called to him. London, Piccadilly. The sunken lanes of Devon. The Yorkshire moors. But he knew that when it was time to come back he would be glad. He had cut himself off from all that. No one would be interested in Africa. No one would bother to pick up the strings of old friendships that would so soon be cut again. He'd end up with other colonials home for a holiday. They'd tell each other stories. He'd see men from Rhodesia, from Kenya, civil servants from West Africa, other men from the Congo — planters, traders. They'd talk about the food they liked and could not get here, the curries, the palm oil chop, the groundnut soups, the fresh coconuts, the pineapples. Now he wanted dressed crab, cold grouse, salmon, oysters and a nice chump chop. But when he'd had them all he'd want his African food again. He'd want the smell of the cookfires, of woodsmoke and rancid fat. Even the smell of the niggers. It got into your blood, into your system. You couldn't just be a man in the street again when you had been a king, a master. When you'd torn down forests and ploughed up virgin land. When you'd counted cattle by the hundred, by the thousand, when you were used to being out in the blue where you acknowledged only the most vestigial authority. They all felt like that. First the excitement of coming home, then the slow descent of boredom, the feeling that you weren't wanted, that you didn't belong among these tame little men and women.

Anyway he had never been understood in England. The British at home had no sense of humor. But he would be busy. Very busy. He had plans. Plans that he'd hardly put into words yet, even to himself.

I was really rather excited about Henry's going. He was getting on my nerves badly. It would be a relief not to have to watch him eat breakfast for a few months. It was the way he ate boiled eggs that got me. He did not crack an egg sharply and then take off its top neatly in one piece. He did not pulverize it and pull off the shell attached to the membrane. He broke it low down so that the yolk always ran out down its side onto the white eggcup and dribbled onto the plate. It was revolting, disgusting.

It was no use saying one shouldn't take a dislike to a man because of the way he ate a boiled egg. One did. One couldn't help it. I had become almost hysterical about it. I tried to avoid him at breakfast but it seldom worked. If I had it late he was late too. I had tried to rationalize it. It's the climate, I thought. Everyone knows what it does to you. Well, even if it was the climate it didn't make things any better. It might explain it but it changed nothing.

I was not worried about taking over from him. I was a good stockman. Not as good as he was. I could never have organized the place but I could keep it running till he got back.

"You'll be lonely," he said.

I said, "I'll manage."

"You've never been alone like this before," he said. "I have and I know what it's like."

"There's Colley," I said, "and Anna."

"Yes," he said, "there's Colley."

I knew he was thinking about Marie-Thérèse, but he didn't mention her. He was more worried about his guns.

"You'll take care of them, won't you? Keep them in grease unless you're using them."

I said, "Yes. I don't suppose I'll want them. I've got my own."

"But nothing heavy," he said.

"No," I said.

"And be careful with bush cow."

I said, "I shan't shoot any buck."

He could never understand why I had given up shooting. I had been in the shooting eight at school too. And a better shot than he was. It had been easier to tell him my eyes had gone, that I could only use a shotgun now, than explain that I had come to hate killing. That I had done too much of it. I knew he was thinking that the guns were valuable, irreplaceable, and that Marie-Thérèse was not. It was a curious thought.

She'd belonged to other white men before. A trader had taken her to Leo, but when Henry came her family had got her back. They were afraid of her becoming a prostitute on her own and keeping her earnings. So when a vacancy, that is to say a white man alone, turned up near home, they sent for her. He had paid her father for her of course, and it would be good to have someone in the white man's house, in his bed, to tell them what he was doing.

That was the way their minds worked. A woman was just a thing. Like a gun, only not worth so much. Their minds and Henry's were at one on this subject. A girl was just so much cash, so many hoes or spears, so many bottles of gin. And with a girl in a white man's house you not only had a spy, but when he went away — and they always went away or died — you could sell her again to someone else. There were great advantages in having an educated daughter. Marie-Thérèse had been brought up in the Convent of the Sacred Heart, fifty miles away. That was where the trader had found her. Yes, a girl like that was a gold mine. Her father was a lucky man.

To her it was all a matter of complete indifference as long as she belonged to a white man who gave her plenty of new pagnes, good food and did not beat her too much. The one thing she would not do was to return to tribal life, to work in the fields and carry wood and water like an animal. She spat when she thought of those black women. Like animals. Monsieur Henri was a good man. He gave her plenty of perfume, kola nuts to chew, cigarettes to smoke and gin when she asked for it. Oh yes, a good man. With whom she slept did not matter. She had no feelings about that. She had been circumcised and got no pleasure. But she had been trained in the Poro bush to give pleasure, before the mission got her. They had taken her late and she had not stayed long. But she had learned some French, how to wash and iron her clothes and eat with implements in the silly way of the white people. She knew Monsieur Henri was going. She supposed Monsieur Jim would take her on. That would be only natural. She hoped Monsieur Henri would bring her back some nice presents — necklaces and brooches, and perhaps some new records for the gramophone.

She had an ambition. It was to be white. She was half white and if she had a baby with a white man it would be whiter than she was. That was what she meant by being white. Until now she had put it off but she would. Oh yes, she would. The time had come.

Her father had been an assistant surveyor who had worked on the road that had never been made. People still laughed about it. It had been begun and then abandoned, and when they had come back later it had gone, swallowed up by the forest. Even the markers they had put in had gone. Naturally they had gone. They were of iron. They had been beaten into spearheads before the white men had been away a week. It was her father, that is to say the husband of her mother, who had sold her mother to the assistant surveyor for, what was in those days, a very good price, and who had arranged for the good sisters to take his child. She is part white, he had said. She must become evolved. That made her laugh. All this evolution. As if women needed it.

It was amusing too to think of her fathers. Her white father, who no doubt was dead by now. Men did not live long in the Congo twenty years ago, and her father in the village, the husband of her mother, to whom she was no relation but to whom she belonged by law.

4 The Letter

These were the people I was living among. This was my life while Henry was away. The usual routine of dipping and counting stock, of paying wages, of doctoring sick cattle, of branding, earmarking, cutting, and weaning calves. I shot an occasional bird. When I wanted meat I got one of the natives to hunt it with an old .303.

The drought broke soon after Henry left. There was no more talk of leopard men. There was no excitement. The days passed, and the nights. Marie-Thérèse made infantile attempts to seduce me. I resisted her without difficulty. Not that she cared, as long as she had food and drink, cigarettes and the gramophone to play. Her efforts had been made without enthusiasm and had been repulsed in the same spirit.

It was curious that the twinges of desire I had had when

Henry was there ceased when he left. I was astonished at my virtue, or was it fastidiousness? Either way the result was the same. I saw a lot of Colley and Anna. Sometimes Anna spent the day with me. I'd ride up to the mission and bring her back with me in front of my saddle. Then Colley would drive over for dinner in his old Ford and take her home.

In my way I was happy, insulated from the outside world with its problems that were beyond my ability to meet. Perhaps it is that — an inability to face modern competitive conditions that sends men to the colonies.

The mornings were often very beautiful. Mist covered the world like a white sea, out of which the little tree-clad hilltops rose like islands. The veld was green. There were wild flowers — gladioli, tall pink orchis and flowering shrubs and trees. Africa was in one of her gentler moods. I should have been warned by this calm-before-the-storm feeling, but I did not know enough then to fear life when there were no troubles. I did not know that the gods tricked men by saving things up, by piling up disasters so that they could let them go in a great avalanche when the moment came. This was what poor Colley was always praying about though he did not realize it. Still he prayed. This was why the Africans, wiser than white men, sacrificed their white cocks and black goats. Why they poured libations of palm wine and trade gin onto the soil, why they spread food between the roots of the great tree buttresses. Why they sacrificed a human being when they could. I did not at that time understand the humor of the gods. No young man does. A young man is like an animal. He does not believe in death or disaster. Whatever happens, he will survive. I did not know that when things are going well you should ride your luck, but go on tiptoe as you do it. That above all a man must never call attention to himself by saying how well things are going. That he must never call things by their right names. The Africans know this. They do not mention the name of the river. They will call it "he that flows." The leopard they call "the spotted one" or "our friend in the forest." That certainly should fool the leopard. When one has lived long enough among them one gets into their ways and begins to think as they do. I still do, to some extent.

The stock had done well. We had had few losses and the head office was very satisfied with my reports. They talked of starting up a new herd in another area. They had more or less offered me the job if they did, and suggested that I might try some experimental oil-palm planting. It sounded very interesting.

I was pleased at how well I stood the solitude. I read a great deal. I tried my hand at writing down some of my impressions. I even sold something to *Blackwood's*. I cut my drinking down to one whiskey and soda before dinner. A man has to be careful about drinking when he is alone. I was careful, too, about my appearance. My baths, my hair that Colley cut for me. I shaved every day and wore clean clothes. It is very easy to let things go. This is the beginning of the road downhill. This is why men on distant stations and isolated posts may solemnly dress for dinner and practice a kind of solitary protocol. It is not a joke, not part of the white man's burden, but a defensive measure against deterioration.

But finally the loneliness of the bush penetrates the heart.

Time is lost in the monotony of the veld. Without society
a man ceases to exist as a man. He is cut off from his past
by the knife of his isolation. He no longer has a bank
balance or an overdraft, no longer has friends or relatives.
He has nothing. Nothing matters. Sometimes he will not
even collect his mail or answer it. He becomes one with
this emptiness, with the beasts that he tends, with the wild
animals, with the savages with whom he shares this vast-
ness. They are all part of a simple plan. He is not a cog in
a machine as he is in the civilized world. He is integrated
into a universe, his personality merged into what is called
nature. And against this is set, or at least it was in my case,
a sense of pent-up strength, of fury, of waiting like a caged
animal for some outlet, for a way out — a waiting for something to happen, a subconscious alertness. In the wilds, till
he loses his temper, a civilized man is compressed like a
coiled spring. He is aware that somewhere in him there
is a trigger and wonders what will set it off. It might have
been Marie-Thérèse. She was beautiful enough in a catlike
way. I think she could have done it if she had really wanted
to. She was just too lazy, and her Monsieur Henri would
soon be back with wonderful gifts from over the sea. But
I had no doubt that she had a talent for sending men mad,
like so many of her golden-colored sisters, when she saw
advantage in it and chose to exert it.

Our homestead was comfortable. Built of whitewashed
mud and poles with a thick roof of thatch that came down
in the front and the back, shading the verandahs like a hat.
There were three rooms. A long living room in the middle
with two bedrooms, one at either end, opening off it. On
the back stoep there was a bathroom and a tiny room that

Marie-Thérèse used when she was not with Henry. She kept it closed. A big galvanized padlock fastened the hasp and staple on the door. She wore the key on a string round her waist, tucked into her loincloth. God knows what treasures she had concealed in there, what loot, what secret pickings besides her pagnes and headcloths, which she kept in a tin trunk that was painted white and spotted with round dots of Reckitt's blue. The houseboys had a hut fifty yards away and the cookhouse stood between the boys' quarters and the back stoep. Behind the boys' house came the horse stable, the storerooms, the dip, the home kraals and the sheds where we could keep any sick beasts under observation. In front we had our garden, which consisted chiefly of flowering trees and shrubs — bohinia, flame trees, pride of Barbados, frangipani, moon flower, hibiscus, poinsettia, all the usual common stuff. Cannas were about the only flowers that grew well or at least that would grow without trouble. Climbing the verandah pillars, bougainvilleas, both red and purple, poured their arterial gushes of color over the thatch. We had never cemented the stoep floor. It was one of those things that was always going to be done and never was done. When we had cement we always used it for something more urgent — the foundations of a building or a stable floor.

Pictorially, the ranch house left little to be desired. It had a kind of exotic, savage, Christmas-card appearance. It stood out like a jewel set in a crown of moss. It was only when you looked closely — and I no longer looked — that you noticed things which are not to be found in a Christmas-card cottage. The white walls were stained red by the veins of the white ants' galleries. We knocked them off almost every day, but they started again, and left behind them the faint, double pink line of their foundations as a reminder of their persistence. Then of course there were scorpions and centipedes and tarantulas and mice and rats; and the occasional snakes that came after the rats. There were insects of various kinds, moths as big as my hand, big blundering beetles, flies and mosquitoes.

But you got used to all these things. Used to shaking out your boots before you put them on. To keeping your eye open for anything unusual, such as a snake coiled up on a chair. That had happened once. But the risks were really negligible. There was much less danger in a month here than in a day in London or New York, where the slightest miscalculation in crossing a road may mean death.

The furniture in the house was better than is usual under such circumstances. Fatty Seaman had taste. The chairs and tables were all of native wood made by African craftsmen at a Catholic mission near Leo. They were dark, almost black, and took a good polish. There were skins on the polished red granolithic floor. Lion, zebra, kudu and sable, which here they call the horse antelope. There was a fine leopard skin with its legs extended nailed to the wall. Other leopard skins hung over the backs of the chairs. The walls were decorated with innumerable trophies of the chase. Horned heads — the whitened skulls, rather sinister with their empty eye sockets, open nostrils and bared teeth. Henry had a gorilla skull and two chimps on a shelf. They looked very human — a continual reminder of our simian past. He got them when he was working in French Territory. I am inclined to think he had killed them himself, although he said he hadn't. Not that his word could always be trusted — but because he was always talking about people who had kept heads they had not shot in a most disparaging manner. On the other hand, he may have denied it because there is a certain prejudice against people who kill anthropoid apes for sport, in addition to its being illegal in all territories except in self-defense. This was of course not only due to their rarity and manlike appearance, but because the natives were very fond of eating them and this, for obvious reasons, was discouraged by the authorities, as they were said to taste like men by those who had eaten both. But it is the lush who always accuses the other people of drunkenness. So I never really made up my mind about it one way or the other. Still, he was a fine shot and hunting was one of his great interests.

Then below the dado of heads and horns was a very decorative arrangement of native weapons. Spears, kerries, shields, knives, machetes, swords and guns. Long-barreled Arab guns bound with brass, dane guns, old tower muskets, ancient elephant guns, and even a blunderbuss.

Anna, when she came, was always fascinated by the heads and weapons. "Daddy has nothing like that," she said.

I said, "Your daddy is a man of peace."

"And aren't you and Uncle Henry?"

It was difficult to explain to a child what the war had done to people like us. Henry had had a natural taste for war, and I had gone into it straight from school. It was my introduction to the adult world, to freedom. Of course I had been frightened, but there had been compensations. A sense of belonging, of comradeship. A curious elation at survival, of living when others died; as if it was a gift, something due to one's own intelligence. In a sense it was.

You became war wise. A man was more likely to be killed in the first three weeks than later in ordinary routine trench warfare. In action it was a matter of luck, but then one always felt oneself lucky. One could not imagine oneself dead. The others, yes, but not me.

That "Uncle Henry" annoyed me too. It was all right my being Uncle Jim. But Henry — I knew she liked me better, but still I was jealous. I wanted to be the only one she loved. As if she could help loving. She loved as she breathed.

I said, "Your father is a fine man and it takes all sorts to make a world."

I could not tell her how I sometimes looked at the weapons and wondered about them. They were not tourist souvenirs. They were the tools of death, working tools like the hammers and chisels of a carpenter, apt to the hands that held them. They aroused a kind of nostalgia for action. For war. I thanked God it was over, that there would be no more wars. But all the same there was a residue, a sediment to my hopes of peace. They were in some way qualified.

We went for a walk round the compound. She liked flowers and clapped her hands with pleasure. I showed her the rock garden I had made, using an outcrop near the compound fence. Beyond it was the bamboo wood, which had a fascination of its own. The clumps grew like giant grasses, which of course they were, arching over the intervening spaces between them, forming little glades.

"There should be fairies, here," she said. "It's a fine place for fairies. I think I should see them if I came in the moonlight."

"You see fairies?" I asked.

"Oh yes, often. They are beautiful."

The john was at the bottom of the garden screened by elephant grass. The gate leading to the rock garden was just beyond it. Sanitation in those days was a primitive affair and there were certain inconveniences in the rainy season in having it outside, although it was not really far — only thirty yards or so from the house.

I remember that day very well because when Colley came to dine and fetch Anna he brought me a letter from Henry.

I opened it at once in case it needed an answer. Colley sent to the Beach quite often. There was quite a coming and going between the mission and the outer world. Africans came for medical treatment, out of curiosity, to see friends, or just for no reason at all.

"Dear Jim" — Henry wrote — "I have some news for you." (There must be news, I thought, because he hardly ever wrote.) "I am married and bringing my wife back in two months time. Please clean the place up. My room and so on, and tidy the compound. Maybe you'd better white-wash the house too." (Maybe I had, I thought.)

The rest was just business about the cattle, and he hoped his guns were not rusting.

I said, "He's bringing back a wife, Colley."

"So he's married," Colley said.

"A girl?" Anna said. "How wonderful — fancy another girl here! Is she white?" she asked.

"Of course she's white," I said.

"It will mean big changes," Colley said.

I knew he meant Marie-Thérèse. She was never mentioned directly between us. She was merely accepted. It was rather the way a house is accepted as being haunted in some village at home. Everyone knows it is, but no one talks about it. After all we only talk about things we are not sure about, arguing the pros and cons.

The next few weeks were busy ones. We had rather let things slide and there were a lot of minor repairs to make. Holes in the walls to be patched, thatch to be replaced. But whitewash covers a multitude of sins. Sometimes I felt the house was supported by its multiple skins of whitewash. I did nothing about Marie-Thérèse. He had not mentioned her. Anyway let him do his own dirtywork. But I had no doubt that she knew.

By the time I took the truck to meet them — how funny the *them* sounded in my ears — the place looked pretty good. I was proud of it. I was not particlularly preoccupied with wondering what she looked like. Or pretended that I wasn't. She, the nameless, faceless, formless one, who was joining us, who lived like castaways on this flower-embowered raft in a jungle sea. The stranger. The woman. She might be anything. I wondered what she would make of it and of us. Our situation was not normal, though one came to accept it. Even without her. With her it became even more abnormal. A woman with two men. A triangle. But nothing like that must happen. I hoped she would not be beautiful. I also hoped she would not be ugly. Not beautiful enough to disturb me, not ugly enough to be unpleasant to look at. I hoped she would have a pretty voice. I was very voice conscious. And now I was going to meet her. There is always some excitement in a man's heart when he goes to meet a strange woman, even if she is another man's wife. I made the boys give the truck a good wash, in spite of knowing that by the time I reached the Beach, it would be as dirty as ever. I shaved more carefully than usual, though I should have to shave again tomorrow before the boat came in. I packed one of my good shirts to put on for the meeting.

5 The Woman

Henry said: "This is Helen."

I said: "Hullo, old boy."

I took her hand and said: "How do you do? I hope you had a good trip."

Her hand was very soft with long fingers. The nails were long, almond-shaped and painted red.

I called the boys to get the gear into the truck. They piled everything in and got in themselves. There was quite a bit of stuff for the ranch at the store, as well as Henry's things. Dip, three bags of concentrates for the bulls, kerosene, paint and a keg of nails. The usual things. But I had loaded them earlier.

I went over to Erikson the captain of the little woodburner that had brought them up the river.

"Hullo," I said.

"Hullo Jim," he said. "Quite a change there'll be now, *hein?* With her in the 'ome, *ja?* A beauty," he said. "He's got himself a beauty. But I wonder how smart it is to do such a thing? And you wonder too, *hein?* Flowers like that grow in the cement, my friend, not in the bush. But it will be to watch interesting, I think — no?"

I said, "Oh yes. Most interesting." I did not really care for Erikson. He was half Swedish and half Dutch. A good man when sober. Therefore seldom a good man. But even drunk he knew his job as a river captain.

A beauty, he'd said. Well, perhaps she was. I hadn't really taken her in. She had not looked at me when we were introduced. Her eyes had been downcast. I'd noticed her long lashes. Her soft hand had seemed boneless in mine. I had an idea of an almost, but not quite, boyish slimness. Maybe I hadn't wanted to notice more.

"Come on!" Henry shouted.

I got into the truck. There was room for us all on the front seat. Henry drove. Helen was next to him and I sat on the outside. There was room, but only just room, and I was very conscious of Helen. Her thigh against mine seemed very soft and warm. I do not know why some women feel warmer than others. I assume they all have normal temperatures of 98.6 but sometimes it doesn't feel like that.

She was wearing a dark blue silk dress with a design of white suns and half-moons on it. She had on no stockings and white buckskin shoes with high heels. She had beautiful legs. They were slim and muscular. Beautiful ankles. A high instep that showed her bones and a faint blue tracery of veins. Round her waist she wore a wide white buckskin belt. The dress was short-sleeved and her arms looked thin and childish. She must be very young, I thought. Her hands lay open, one on top of the other, on her lap. I looked at her face. Erikson had been right — she was a beauty.

She had taken off her hat, a white double terai. Her hair, which had a natural wave, was long, ash blond, with patches of a lighter shade. She turned towards me. Her eyes met mine. They were big, grey, and set very far apart in a heart-shaped face. Her mouth was wide but pretty and sensitive when she smiled. She had small, very even, very white teeth.

Then she looked away again, staring ahead down the track. So this is Helen, I thought. The girl whose room I had got ready. I thought of the flowers I had put on her dressing table. I had done it as a kind of joke. I had had no idea what sort of woman Henry would bring back but I had not expected anyone like this. I had not wanted anyone like this. Any woman would have been a disturbing factor in our little ménage. Marie-Thérèse hadn't counted that way. But this was going to be more than a disturbing element.

I wondered how Henry had got her. Erikson was right. She was a city girl. A flower of the pavements. How would she stand transplantation?

The trip was curiously silent. None of us spoke much. Each was occupied with his or her own thoughts.

Henry said: "Everything all right?"

I said: "Yes."

He said: "No losses?"

"Only the normal," I said.

"Wild, isn't it, Helen?" Henry said.

She said: "Yes, you told me it would be." She had a soft voice.

I wondered if he'd told her how wild it really was. How isolated.

I said: "I fixed up your room. I put in flowers."

She said: "Thank you. How kind you are."

I didn't feel kind.

The trip took six hours. I had come the day before and slept in the truck to meet the boat at the landing. Pedro, the Portuguese half-caste who kept the store, had entertained me. On the way back we had a picnic lunch and stopped a couple of other times to stretch our legs. When I'd seen Helen look about in a rather hopeless sort of way and then start off towards the bush I told her to wait till I'd gone ahead to have a look around.

There was no point in being modest about these things. When I came back Henry said, "Quite a ladies' man, aren't you?"

I thought he should have done it himself, but didn't say so. Instead I said, "She's not used to things yet. Suppose there was a snake or something?"

"Not likely," he said. "There are not so many snakes."

"I know," I said, "but there might be. Or ants."

The idea of ants seemed to amuse him.

We saw one kudu and Henry said it was a pity I hadn't brought a rifle. I only had the shotgun but I had some buckshot cartridges which would kill anything at close range if there was trouble.

I tried to imagine what a city-bred girl would think of

the bush we were driving through. Harsh savannah, open plains, patches of dark, primary forest. Nothing that resembled in any way what we call the country at home. Not even the moors had this savagery, or bleakness. The grass was not like our grass, the trees not like our trees. Most of them, except in the forest, gave no shade. And in the forest there was no light. Many of them had thorns. Some were poisonous.

Helen seemed to take it all as a matter of course, and expressed neither interest nor surprise, even at some of the naked Africans we met on the road.

I think she was too tired to really take things in, or that her capacity for surprise was used up. Everything, including the voyage, must have been so new and strange that the bowl of her interest was full to overflowing. There was no room for anything more in it.

At last we got home. When we could see the house I pointed it out to her.

"There you are!" I said.

"That's Lukika," Henry said.

"How pretty it is!" she said.

And it was, in the light of late afternoon, on fire with bougainvillea, golden shower and cannas.

I helped her down from the truck. Henry came out heavily. In the Congo most people either put on weight or lose it. Very few people keep their normal weight. Always fat, he was now gross. He had put on more weight on his holiday. Marriage fattens some men.

I led the way. She followed me. Then Henry came, and after him the boys with the luggage. The big living room looked very comfortable and homey. I had put flowers there too. I was glad to see they had lasted. I flung open the door of Henry's room.

"Your room," I said.

I left her at the door as Henry reached us. I called to the boy to bring hot water and the drinks.

"Dinner in an hour," I said. "Is that all right for you?"

"That's fine," Henry said. Then he said, "You've done a good job with the house."

I said, "Thanks." I was glad. Not that I gave a damn what he thought really. I had done it because he had told me to and he was the boss. But I was glad now that I had made such a good job of it for the kid. She wouldn't feel quite so lost. I only hoped there were no accidents for a few days. None, till she had settled down a bit. By accidents I meant the little things we had got so used to that we hardly mentioned them. If I killed a scorpion in my room I never said anything about it. After all what did I expect to find?

When they came out they had both changed. Henry into the usual khaki shirt and trousers, Helen into a white frock that made her look even more fragile and ethereal. We had drinks. Whiskey and soda. She didn't like whiskey so I gave her a Dubonnet. I don't think she liked that either, but she needed something to pick her up. We had roasted peanuts and biscuits spread with tinned cheese.

Then we had dinner. I was rather proud of it all. The look of the house, my catering arrangements. The dinner began with chicken broth — about all the local chickens were fit for — fish from the river — rather bony but still edible — and bush fowl cooked with red wine. I'd shot them before I left yesterday. They were really francolin —

double-spurred Senegal francolin — rather like large partridges. We call our local variety pheasants in South Africa. The sweet was a jelly which had not set properly, and canned cream. It made a rather pretty mush that looked like strawberries and cream and tasted of raspberries. We ended up with coffee. We drank the red Portuguese wine with the meal that we got in bulk from Pedro.

There was very little conversation. What should have been a festive meal, the first of a bride in her new home, did not work out that way. Henry was pompous and talked about the people he'd met and the shows he'd seen. Helen said practically nothing.

I asked her where she came from.

She said, "Bournemouth."

Henry confirmed it by saying, "Yes, she comes from Bournemouth."

I said, "I like Bournemouth. There's some very pretty country round about."

Henry said, "I don't think she saw much of the country." And that ended that.

I tried to place her. But it's hard to place people who don't say anything. She ate nicely but stuck out her little finger when she drank. She called a napkin a serviette and so that took her out of the top drawer. I do not know if I was unconsciously snobbish. I don't think so. She was too pretty, enchantingly so, for me to have cared. It was just that I wanted to know all I could about her. I couldn't understand how Henry had found her, or why she had married him. At that time I don't suppose, excluding missionaries, there were a hundred women in the whole Colony.

I decided she might have worked in a shop or beauty

parlor, or have been a typist. A typist would be useful on the ranch.

After dinner we sat around and had a few more drinks. We had whiskies again and I introduced Helen to grenadine and soda. She sat very still sipping her drink and smoking a cigarette in a long imitation-amber holder.

She jumped when a big beetle crashed into the lamp and fell on the floor near her. I picked him up and chucked him outside. I thought it was a pity that the first one should be so big. White, with black stripes, a Goliath, about the size of a golf ball. Rather rare as a rule. I did not kill him, partly because I don't like killing things and partly because if I'd squashed him on the floor the way I might have done had we been alone, the noise of his being mashed and the mess might have upset her.

It would be interesting to see the effect she was going to have on our behavior. A civilizing influence, I thought. All civilization, when one came to think about it, was dependent on women. On mothers and wives. It was they who insisted on neatness, cleanliness and good behavior. They set the standards at home which might be why most of us were so relieved to go back to the wilds again. But it would be interesting to see what happened here now.

I had not seen Marie-Thérèse, but I was sure she had seen us. She might even be outside now, looking in. Everything is seen in Africa, or almost everything. There are always sharp black eyes watching from behind some bush, or from the long grass. No strange animal is more observed than the white man in Africa. Our actions fascinate and interest the black people. Nothing is too mad for a white man to do. No action too strange. Above all, they love to see us wash, to note the whiteness of our skins when we strip, in contrast to our sunburned faces, necks, hands and arms. They think we are very ugly, resembling the dead in our pallor.

Then I wondered what she was thinking. This was in a sense the classic colonial triangle — the white man who brings home a white wife and discards his native mistress. I could foresee, or rather feel, the possibility of another triangle in which I would figure with Henry and Helen. This was something I wanted to avoid. I didn't want to become involved. But it was a long time since I had seen anyone so lovely. It was not just that it was a long time since I had seen a white woman — Helen would have been remarkable anywhere. She had the quality that would make men turn and look back over their shoulders if they passed her in any street. The quality that makes men feel they have missed something. That their lives are drab.

I determined to have as little to do with her as possible. Only trouble could come of it if I messed about with her. Besides, I was afraid of Henry. He could have smashed me with one blow of his great fists, the way I could smash a beetle. And there was my job to consider. I did not put it past him to queer my pitch with the company. To say I drank, or was not to be trusted with money, and prevent my getting anything else to do in the Colony, if he caught me making a pass at his wife.

I had hardly made these resolutions when a sausage fly landed on Helen's lap. I picked it off and squashed it on the floor. She had not moved, but I saw her bite her lip. That touch had set me on fire. To pick it up I'd had to press my fingers into the soft flesh of her thigh.

Henry said, "You'll have to learn to do that sort of thing for yourself, and remember, if ever you get a centipede on you, brush it forward, not back."

"Forward?" she said.

"Yes darling. The way it's going. If you don't it'll sting you with all its legs."

He looked very bland. His face was red with drink and the sun. His shining hair was almost white in the half-lit room.

What's the matter with him, I thought. He's torturing her. God knows the place was odd enough as far as she was concerned, without that. The horns on the wall threw twisted shadows, the weapons, where they caught the light, shone menacingly. And outside, the damn tam-tams were louder than usual. Then they stopped and a big drum began to beat. You could feel it, as much as hear it. The dull throb vibrated in the room, as if it was a soundbox. It was like the war. Where one felt the big guns before one heard them.

"What's that, Henry?" she asked.

"Talking drums," he said.

"What are they saying?"

"No idea," he said. "But I can guess. They are talking about you. Saying that I have brought back a white wife from over the sea."

"Strange place, isn't it?" I said. "But you'll get used to it. There's nothing to worry about."

"What does one do here?" she asked.

"Do?" Henry said. "Nothing. There's nothing to do."

"No people?"

"No one but us," he said, "and old Colley at the mission."

She said, "Oh, I see." Then she said, "I know you told me it was lonely, but I'd no idea it was quite so far from everything."

I knew what she meant by everything. The shops. The pictures. The pavements. She had never been anywhere where there was nothing before.

"We're on our own here," Henry said.

I had been more or less right in my guess about Helen. Her father had been the accountant to some small firm of importers in the city of London. He had died without having made any provision for his wife and daughter. His insurance had been allowed to lapse. My own idea was that he had tried to live at a far higher rate than was justified by his earnings, in the hope that Helen would make a good marriage. Everything had been sacrificed to appearances. Once she was safe he would be able to relax and live simply. Unfortunately he'd popped off before this happened. His wife soon followed and, after trying several jobs, in each of which men — both the managers and the patrons — had made passes at her, Helen had cashed in on the one thing she did really well — dancing. She had been very well taught and became a dance hostess and taxi dancer. Now at least if passes were made she got paid for them. My feeling was that by the time Henry met her she was several men away from being a virgin.

Once I got it figured out I was not surprised. He could never have got an ordinary, respectable girl to marry him. He could never have taken a girl who had parents off to the Congo after a few weeks acquaintance.

Helen had not been particularly interested when the fat

fair man in a dinner jacket had asked for a dance. She'd said, "Thank you, I'd like to dance." That was what she was paid to do. He had his ticket in his hand. He had bought the right to hold her in his arms as long as they kept moving, to tread on her feet, even to fumble around a bit and to make veiled, or not-so-veiled, suggestions about afterwards. It was all routine. She knew all the lines. Nothing could surprise her now.

But he did. First by the way he danced. It was like dancing with another professional. Suddenly, incredible as it might seem, she was enjoying dancing again. Something she had never believed possible.

And then he had proposed. Proposed not a night in an hotel, not a weekend somewhere, but marriage.

He'd said, "And what is your name, young lady?"

She'd said, "Helen."

He said, "Well Helen, I am only in England for a few more weeks and I would like to see something more of you. If we get on I would like you to be my wife."

"You mean marry you?"

"That's what I mean. It's lonely in Africa. But it might be an improvement on this. Unless you like all this sort of thing?"

He had let go of her right hand to wave round the floor at the collection of sweating men, and tired, almost pretty girls who circled them.

"I don't know," she said. "It's very sudden, isn't it?"

"Love at first sight," he said.

"You dance very well," she said.

"Henry the name is," he said. "Henry Seaman, at your service!"

He succeeded in inclining his body towards her as they danced. Clumsy as a bear when walking, Henry was remarkable when dancing, a miracle of speed and grace. He might have had built-in skates on his feet as he swept along, floated and turned. He was rather like a polar bear when it gets into the water. It is no longer the same animal. He was the same when he fought. I'd seen him in one or two roughhouses. Then this great lump of lard was suddenly metamorphosed into a cannon ball of energy that bounced and struck with almost incredible speed. He seemed to have a reserve of energy that he could turn on like a tap. He had only two speeds. Low, and a kind of extra high, souped-up top, with unbelievable acceleration, so that he jumped from the one into the other without any apparent gearshift. Emotionally he was the same, and when he had turned the full power of his charm and personality onto this pretty, rather shopworn and lonely little creature, he swept her off her feet and into his bed in a series of small hotels; and, when he found her satisfactory there, to a registry office, where he took out a license to sleep with her anywhere, at any time, in much the same spirit as he would have taken out a license for a dog that he had bought because its appearance had pleased him and he enjoyed its tricks.

But to her he was Prince Charming. He was Perseus to her Andromeda, delivering her, cutting the pink chains of those rolls of tickets that had chained her to the rock of exhausting indignity. It was Henry's chance to be worshipped.

She had been at it long enough to know how lucky a dance hall girl was to get married to anyone. Anyone at all.

There was only one other way out. To be kept for a while and then find oneself being handed on from one man to another, till finally the last man sold you to his acquaintances, or sent you out onto the streets.

Henry had made the Congo sound so romantic. Made himself sound so fine. A pioneer, an explorer. He talked of thousands of hectares.

"What's a hectare?"

"Two acres approximately."

That made a hectare somehow so much more exciting than two acres. She had no real idea what an acre was, but she'd learned about them at school. There were so many — she forgot how many — square yards in an acre. And there were six hundred and forty acres in a square mile. She'd remembered that but she'd never really understood what a square mile was. A mile was long. It was what you walked, and two of them were enough for anyone.

She knew very little about London. Hardly anything about the West End, the theatres, the shops, Bond Street or the rest. The London of clubs and luxury flats, of Rotten Row and Green Park. Her home had been in the suburbs, in Golders Green. Her jobs had been in Kensington. I never found out how she had got down to Bournemouth. Probably some man took her there and ditched her. I never asked her any questions. What I found out was by indirection, by putting the little things she said together and making a picture of her life. Anyway I saw as little of her as I could. Which was not easy, living in the same house and not wanting to hurt her by avoiding her too obviously.

I had the feeling that Henry was watching me. Or us. Playing a kind of cat-and-mouse game. Dangling sexual opportunity before us as if it were a carrot.

I never really understood Henry. He had, as I have said, this passion for practical jokes. He seemed completely indifferent to other people's feelings, and although one knew this, it was hard to feel that he really meant any harm. I was at that time still suffering from the Falstaff delusion. That the fat are really good-natured. God knows Henry smiled and laughed enough.

I think he wanted a situation to develop so that he could exploit it in some peculiar, humorous fashion. I do not think he would have minded being a cuckold. I could even see his point of view. She had not been new when he got her. A woman was not a postage stamp that could only be used once. If we fell for each other he would have more power over both of us. A whip he could crack. Particularly if we did not know whether he knew or not. If we were uncertain. It was not a healthy situation, nor one that could have occurred under different conditions. But the conditions of equatorial Africa are not normal. Nor are the people who find themselves there. At least they weren't then. Now, I understand it has a very high standard of morality.

There were so many factors to be balanced, to be equated. The climate. The solitude. The Africans. Our own characters. Henry the farmer's son who, after a distinguished war career, had come to grief in the great white lights of London and gone farming in the Congo. I who, with a less distinguished war record and mixed farming and other experiences in South Africa, Portuguese East and Rhodesia, had joined him in this venture. Our tie being the almost forgotten school days which we had shared and the fact that we were both ex-officers. We were neither of us ambitious. We just wanted to be left alone, to go our own way, even if it was downhill.

And then Helen. A little suburban miss who, through no fault of her own, had become a floosie.

Add Marie-Thérèse, the discarded African girl, to the mixture. Add tam-tams, talking drums, tales of human leopards, cannibals, ritual murders, hot moonlit nights, fire-flies, the maddening metronome squeak of the fruit bats, the maniac cries of the tree bears, the croaking of the frogs, the laughing cries of the hyenas, the roar of lions, the cough of a leopard, snakes, insects; rains of unbelievable icy violence, which made one shiver while they fell, and then when the sun came out again, cooked one in the steaming heat of their evaporation. Storms that swept down upon us, tornadoes that attacked patches of forest, picking up trees and huts as if they were children's toys, or ripped a sudden path through the impenetrable bush.

These were the forces that played upon us like the spot-lights of a theatre on the principals. But here we were all principals. Each playing his part in a drama whose plot none of us knew.

To keep my mind off Helen I approached Marie-Thérèse. I found it less hard than I had imagined. While Henry was away I had not touched her, but now, excited by the white woman, the mood was too strong to be killed by so small a thing as color. As if she knew my mind, Marie-Thérèse drenched herself in perfume that she stole from Helen. So the two girls smelled the same. And what girl is white in the night?

6 The Storm

Of course there were thunderstorms in Golders Green. There are storms everywhere. Helen's father used to say, "There is going to be a thunderstorm. We must bring in the garden chairs." The garden, of course, was a patch of grass about half the size of a tennis court. Before a storm it was hot, oppressive, and the sky darkened. Then there were some claps of thunder and rain fell. Hard rain for England, which bashed the fuller-blown roses into their integral petally parts. There were always a lot of worms on the lawn after a storm and sometimes a bird was killed, but only young and foolish birds, unstormwise, fell before it. So when we told her there would be a storm in a few days she had seemed glad.

"It will break the heat, won't it?" she said, wiping some beads of sweat away from her forehead.

"What we need is a fan — if we had electricity," Henry said.

I said, "Yes. Like having bacon and eggs for breakfast if we had any bacon." We had tried bacon but it always went rancid.

But our storms were not like that. They had personality. They were savage expressions of God's wrath. First, he sent heat. Unbearable heat, that was so filled with electricity that every nerve was set on edge. The heat was an invisible, smothering blanket. It was as hot at night as in the day, for in the night the ground gave up its heat. And all the time, day and night, men sweated, were wakened by the sweat running down their backs, running between their breasts, between their thighs. Then we used a Dutch wife, a kind of bolster that you hold in your arms and stuff between your legs, blotting up your sweat like blotting paper, absorbing the spilled, colorless, acrid-smelling ink of your body. Before you get your shirt on, it sticks to you. It is black with sweat. One does not perspire in Africa. The word is too weak. Sweat is too weak. Then there is the madness of prickly heat. And the extra salt you must eat to compensate for the salts you lose, that are carried off by the tides of your own moisture. Waterless, your kidneys shrivel. The heat is too great for urine. The normal processes of the body fail. A man is a living colander.

The sky is still cloudless. Then small clouds, like scattered sheep on a blue pasture, appear. They are the heralds. They amalgamate, form platoons, companies, pile themselves into voluptuous, dangerous armies. They are still white, but gold-tipped, with tinges of red as if touched with blood. They pile themselves ever higher as if in anger.

They darken into grey, into purple, with rage. They are suffused, like the face of an angry man. Soon they cover the sky. And it is dark. The morning is like evening. We move through this hot gunmetal-colored world with a sense of unreality, of impending doom. We do not feel that our God, our Christ, operates here — not in this Africa. Perhaps he must have churches and cathedrals of stone in which to live. There are few buildings of stone in Africa and none are ancient, except a few ruins whose origin remains in doubt.

No, these are not our gods. Suddenly we understand why the Africans sacrifice goats, and cattle, and men. Their gods demand blood, will be satisfied with nothing less. The sky comes down nearer to the earth, brooding over it like some gigantic, dark, grey-feathered fowl. Then everything is still. Even the cicadas are hushed. The birds fly no longer for they think that night is coming and seek their perches.

Poor Helen was less happy about the storm now. It was not like storms at home. Nor was this hush before it. It was not a hush. It was a kind of death. Her pink dress was stained dark purple with her girl sweat. Under the arms, on the back, on her thighs. Sweat ran down her face. She rubbed it out of her eyes. When she put up her hands it ran in little drops, hanging on the peach down of her forearms and, gathering strength, raced in rivulets down to the bend of her elbows. We all smelled of sweat. Her perfume did not disguise it. It only made it female. The chair backs were black with it. The leopard skins, where we had leaned against them, matted.

Everything was battened down as far as it was possible. Nothing was left loose about the place. A sheet of corrugated iron, picked up by the wind, would cut a man in two like a great flat sword. I had seen it happen.

The sky darkened to indigo, the horizon became red. The red blended with the almost navy blue of the clouds, into sepia. The wind was coming. The storm always rode the wind as if it were a horse, a great stallion. The red was the dust of its gallop as it tore over the veld. We could hear it come, screaming, whistling. The doors and windows were closed but some got in. Stragglers of wind, as it were. The house seemed to rock, to crouch under the onset. It seemed to realize what a small, man-made thing it really was when confronted with the exaggerated elements.

Outside the trees whipped and then bent almost double, like slaves beneath the scorpion whips of the wind which stripped them naked, violently, as men in haste might strip women taken in a raid. The air was full of leaves and driven rubbish. A hawk, the master of the peaceful air, was flung like a blowing newspaper against a tree. Branches were torn off with great strips of bark, like skin, still hanging to them. There was distant thunder that rolled like the drum-fire of cannon. Oh, this was war! A war of elementals. Of the air gods against the earth gods. Of all the gods combined against mankind. Then came the smell of sulphur, of brimstone, as if the gates of hell had been opened. It came the way the smell comes up out of the subway, all penetrating. It swept through the house. Helen cried out.

"It smells of sulphur!" she said.

I knew she wanted to come to my arms, and since she could not she crouched in her chair, drawing up her legs so that I could see the underside of her childish thighs. She made herself as small as she could. She was shaped like an egg, like a curled foetus, when the rain came. It struck us like a hammer, an iron blow of a hundred million driven drops, welded by the storm into solidity. Suddenly we were fish incisted in a capsule in a raging tank. Outside it was all water. There was no room for air. In the room we could hardly breathe, and then it grew cold. The heat had gone, killed by the violence of the tempest. Nothing, not even heat, could stand against it. The sweat on us turned icy. We shivered.

Overhead the thunder exploded, shaking the house, vibrating through it. Clap on clap, explosion on deafening explosion. The ears no longer heard them. They were only felt. Outside it was light with the blue of the lightning that came down all round us, audibly hissing like gigantic snakes, striking wildly at the unwilling earth, driving electricity, driving life into it, as if it was a womb. Then for an instant it would be darker than night by contrast, and then the darkness was split again, riven by the zigzag forks of lightning that smashed the sky, shattering it like a plate with a pattern of awful cracks.

In the forest, I knew, the great trees were shivering, unable to bend. The oldest would break and fall, their crash inaudible in the roar of the storm. Others would strain at the lianas that held them, as the masts of a ship whip and strain at the rigging in a storm at sea. The savage leopards would be crouched, frightened as fawns, with flattened ears, in their lairs, their spotted fur black with moisture. The buck, too, would be lying pressed down into the grass with fear. Only the lions, kings of the storm, would be on the move, stalking on great soft pads through the rain. The great yellow lions, their mouths half open, their thorn-tipped tails flicking, happy with thoughts of the hot arterial blood and meat that would come to them so easily on a night like this.

Then, as suddenly as it had come, the storm was over. There was only silence, broken by Helen's sobs and the sound of rushing water. The whole world was weeping. The earth, the girl. Every path was a stream, every stream a river, every river a raging torrent. The trees were dripping their tears.

I got my jacket and found coats for Helen and Henry, and sat down. I felt a great emptiness. A great desire for my love, to hold her, to touch her. I knew she was my love now. I had read her thoughts which, liberated by fear, had flown like suddenly released birds from the cage of her heart. Only in a woman can a man find release for his fear. And I had been frightened too. Only a fool is not frightened when so near to the gods. I wanted her warmth, her softness. The feeling that she was more frightened than I, that I could comfort her. Perhaps courage depends upon the fear of others.

All night the water ran, draining away from the high ground. The morning light showed a pulpy world, a green, mashed spinach-like world of flattened grass and fallen leaves that began, with the sun's first heat, to rot. The earth was coated with a rotting, steaming sponge. And as one thing rotted others grew. Everything started to grow now — fantastically, obscenely. Great, fat, leeklike shoots sprang up from hidden bulbs, tree buds burst open into new leaves and blossoms, the palms unsheathed their new green swords and daggers. It was a green, growing world, curiously sinister, livid with menace. It was as if the earth felt it must cover itself quickly with a new skin of foliage to protect its nakedness. So it grew scar tissue — shaggy, tough, like a lion's mane, like the tufts on his elbows. This was the earth. And its denizens, no less hysterical, plunged into an orgy of mating. The birds, the beasts, the butterflies. The insects increased. Thousands of beetles appeared, as if released by the opening of a door. There were flies by the thousand. Great caterpillars crawled over the glaucous leaves, or hung their nets over gigantic trees, covering them, like the furniture of an empty house, with fibrous sheets. There were clouds of ants that seethed in nuptial flight. The wild bees swarmed and began new nests in the hollow trees. They nested in the buildings and had to be destroyed with fire. Hornets built their mud castles, and savagely defended them, in every corner. With the rest of nature, man's blood, too, pounded in his veins.

The night thoughts persisted into the day, became day dreams, day nightmares, that tore the bowels apart with an intolerable mating hunger, that Marie-Thérèse calmed but neither allayed nor satisfied. Smooth as soft black satin; warmly moist, female, she was not to me woman, not the desire of my heart or mind. For this is the white man's curse, that he must think of his love between the satisfactions of his lust. That his love, like his God, is omnipresent. In all things. The fork he uses may have been in her mouth. Her hand had touched the doorknob. The same fingers that have touched his body. Her name occurs in a book and twists his heart into a knot. The lipstick on a cup edge or a cigarette stub is invested with romance.

Marie-Thérèse was not my love, my woman. She was my failing, something I resisted till the zenith of unbearable desire was reached. Then I was disgusted. And then, slowly, as desire mounted again, I remembered the release she offered, the door to peace and sleep that she opened. So it went, the graph of my lust rising and falling in waves, like a slowly mounting and descending fever chart. Like the loops of a fast-moving snake. There was nothing admirable about it. Nothing innocent. Nothing in which it differed from the animal loves of the beasts, or of the Africans themselves, except that I knew what I did as I did it, and afterwards also. My life was one long reproach.

It is seldom understood how life in Africa tests men. That is its charm, its danger, its attraction. Living in Africa is rather like a war. It brings out the hidden weaknesses in a man. It is a continuous challenge. At home men and women can go through life without ever knowing if they are brave or cowardly, honest or thieves, kind or cruel. Life does not really touch them. At home temptation seldom hangs like a fruit, ready to the hand. At home there are alternatives. In Africa there is no choice. It is a matter of doing something or dying, or going mad. Weakness and vice flourish in its soil, sending down their roots into the slime of the ancient past, for a modern man has no place here. He is not wanted. Africa is the land of deterioration, of rusts and molds, of consuming heat which does not purify.

My desire was for Helen. It was now no use my trying to avoid this truth. So that which was aroused by one woman was spent upon another. Because I could not grow roses, I planted the seeds of the thistle. Each time I took the black woman I committed adultery against the white. In trying to save myself I destroyed myself in this land of heat and paradox.

I think Henry knew and enjoyed it, for he took great

pains not to hide their intimacies. It amused him to torture me and see me turn to his discarded mistress for release. And he did not only torture me. Helen loved me. Since the night of the storm she had been unable to disguise her feelings. We looked at each other and away again. We approached each other and then turned back before it was too late.

7 The Beach

So our life continued, superficially normal. Each of us living his own life, in the circle of his own thoughts, and upon each impinged the circles of the others. Our lives were like little adjacent heaps of pennies into which the lives of the other pennies cut at different levels. I have seen pennies, big English ones, built up like this around the edge of a glass. Helen's life was cut into by mine and by Henry's. Mine by Helen's and Henry's. Henry's by Helen's and mine. Marie-Thérèse cut by mine, by Henry's, by Helen's and the life of her tribe. All at different levels, all penetrating to different depths. We were surrounded, hemmed in by the world about us, but continued to live isolated and lonely lives except at these various points of contact. This is no doubt true everywhere, but it is more apparent when a few people are living in isolated situations.

Life would seem to be an attempt to rationalize such pressures, to create a pattern, a comprehensible and comprehensive design in which each man spends his time trying to put his own little house in order, like a hostess preparing her home for guests.

And if I had been thinking less of myself I suppose I should have tumbled to things sooner. I mean I should have seen something was up when there were so many more insects and lizards in the house than was usual, particularly as they were always in the sitting room or in Henry and Helen's bedroom. It had taken me some time to persuade Helen that the almost transparent beige-colored geckos were nice friendly little things that lived on mosquitoes, moths and flies. I told her that all lizards in Africa were harmless, but she really had a terror of them.

One thing that should have opened my eyes was that a number of these lizards, the ordinary, shiny, rather snaky kind such as we have at home, that we found in the house, had no tails. Why should the lizards in the house have no tails? Why, in fact, should these lizards, which are not like geckos or the big agama house lizards, be in the house at all? They like rocks and stones. And certainly, although it did not strike me at the time, a big chameleon, the most terrifying-looking, but the slowest and most harmless of all reptiles, will never come into a house on his own. But one did.

It was all made quite clear one afternoon when, going out for some reason instead of sleeping as I generally did for an hour after lunch, I saw Henry pounce like a great cat on a lizard at the bottom of the garden. I did not show myself but waited to see what he would do. He put it into a small tin box that he brought from his pocket. Giving him time to get back, I went down to where he had been. One of the aloes was in flower. A tall, scarlet candelabrum on which a sunbird was clinging, sucking the nectar from its blooms with a long curved beak. It was a lovely picture — the tiny black, ruby-throated bird, the flower stem that rose out of its sculptured spiky leaves.

There were lots of lizards about here, though. I had never really noticed them before. This must be Henry's hunting ground. I tried to catch one but missed. That he could catch them was just another proof of his deft quickness. But on the ground beside my knee was a lizard's tail. It was still twitching with a life of its own.

Now I had the secret, the explanation. This was another of his little jokes.

I did not go straight back to the house. I did not want Henry to know I had been out. So I went to the stables and drifted round the kraals to look at the sick bull we had there and were trying to get into condition. He was no fatter.

There was no law against a man scaring his wife. There was even no evidence that he did. I was the only witness. If I had been bigger than he was, or even the same size, I might have chanced a row. But could you have a row with another man about his wife? And what about the job? If I got sacked it would be even worse for her. While I was here perhaps I could temper the wind in a way. But what way? The only thing I could think of was to concentrate on teaching her that lizards were nice little things, that they were the friends of man, and eat a lot of nasty things. One rather thought in childish terms when talking to Helen. Nice things. Nasty things.

That evening Henry said, "You'd better take the truck up

to the store tomorrow. There's some stuff there for us."

I said, "All right." I was only too pleased to get out of this atmosphere for a couple of days.

Things were not going at all well with me. I wanted to be with Helen but avoided her, which hurt her feelings. Marie-Thérèse had suddenly become jealous of the attention I paid to Helen. I was in the doghouse with Anna too. She was jealous of Helen and must have heard some servants' gossip about Marie-Thérèse which, with her mission background, made her feel that I was beyond the pale. She varied between trying to save me — a difficult thing for a child of eleven to do — and ignoring me as beyond redemption. She would not ride with me anymore. Said she was too big. But I knew she didn't like my arm round her now. She was becoming a woman, and learning that women do not like their gentlemen friends to have other women in their lives. The friendship she had hoped for with Helen had never matured. It had been stillborn.

It might be flattering to have them all upset about me, but it was far from comfortable. A couple of days shoving the old truck along the bush tracks, and a night with Senhor Pedro da Costa at the Beach might cheer me up. If I bought a couple of new pagnes for Marie-Thérèse it would keep her quiet for a bit. Cloths and beads and brooches — those things were the language she talked. Like most of her kind, she was a born blackmailer. Not only with white men. With Africans even the bride price never seems to be completely paid. The wife goes home in a sulk at intervals and her father demands more gifts before he will exert his influence to send her back again. Of course, in theory, the man can divorce her, get his bride price back and use it to buy a new girl, but in practice it does not work out that way. There is too much delay and litigation before he gets his refund, and his wife takes the children. They are hers, and he has no one to cook for him. To work in his fields. No one to sleep with or sell to his friends when he wants some pocket money. No children to sacrifice for him should he die suddenly.

But it all works out very nicely in the end as long as the man pays up. I was going to pay.

In his hut the chief was looking at his hats. There was the bead-covered skullcap ornamented with the two cow horns, rather like a Viking's helmet, covered with small bright colored beads — wampum, horns and all — which he wore when seeing white men in his official capacity. He wasn't terribly attached to this hat. It was the other that he liked, which few white men had seen. It was made of woven string net to which were fastened dozens of bright red polly feathers, and round the edge, so that they dangled over his face and neck, were pierced leopard fangs.

The witch doctor was with him, looking taller and more shriveled than ever.

"Well, we got rain last season," he said. "Plenty of rain. No one discovered anything and I have some strong medicine left."

The chief took snuff and put his hat back on the crossbeams of the hut.

"We had rain," he said. "You have medicine. There was the stranger and we have got rid of one goat without hair, that gave neither milk nor flesh." He meant a useless member of the tribe. "And the white man has discovered nothing, which proves how good your medicine is. The noise of its virtue goes abroad. I have had offers."

"They will pay much?"

"They will pay very highly." The chief offered his snuff-box. It was made of an old cartridge case. The witch doctor took some from the little bone spoon that was attached to the stopper. He sniffed appreciatively.

"You shall have more," he said.

A child came in. "Lord," he said, "one of them has gone in truck." Everything the white man did was reported.

The drive to the Beach was a cross between a chore and joyride. It was an escape for thirty hours or so. An escape from worry, from embarrassment, from fear, from love. As I piloted that damn truck, which rolled like a ship in the rough seas of the track, I had time to reflect, to sort something out, to plan, to rearrange my feelings into some sort of order, without anyone impinging on me at a critical moment.

First, what did I want? I wanted Helen. But also I didn't want her, partly because of the trouble there'd be. I was afraid of that. And partly because I didn't want to get tied up with her, or with anyone else for that matter, at present. I knew that if I did get mixed up with her it would be bad. I was like that. Boots and all. And she had all the qualities which appealed to both the worst and the best in me. She was, or would be I was sure, sexually maddening, with her hot, soft, flesh; her slim boneless body fitted close against my own. It had not happened yet but that's the way I knew it would be. I could feel her against me in my mind. On the other hand, she appealed to all that was chivalrous in me, to my protective side, to the latent Saint George of the boy that I had once been. The only thing she did not do was to make any sense whatsoever. There was nothing rational about it. She would not make a good wife. I did not want a good wife. She would not make a good mother to the children I did not want. She would not mend the socks I did not wear. Apart from her being married to a man much bigger than I was, and his being my boss. But common sense had no application here. It was not a question of square pegs in round holes, or round pegs in square holes, for any of us. There were no holes quite our shape out here. There was no need for holes. You just drove yourself into the ground and made it fit. You might damage yourself a bit in the process if the ground was hard, red laterite, or fit very loosely if it was the soft mucky humus of the forest. But one way or another you fitted, even if it did not last.

So much for Helen. I had not advanced very much there. Marie-Thérèse came next. She was simpler. A black gold digger, who acted like a bitch in heat. But there was something on her mind. There was some hidden motive. Like most evolved Africans and half-castes, she was a split personality. Presumably she hated white men but, being part white, she could not be assimilated by her mother's people. So she was still more split. She was divided both vertically and horizontally; physically in her blood, culturally in her beliefs, in her hopes and desires. Forced by circumstance to emulate what she hated. She hated Helen but copied her. She hated her tribal relations but was tied to them by the umbilical cord of her upbringing, by her vestigial belief in witchcraft and the never-to-be-forgotten fears implanted in her at her initiation.

The relationship of the two girls was most curious. I had no idea what Helen thought of her, or of her position in the household before she had come. But it must have been fairly near to the truth.

Marie-Thérèse had refused to go home when Helen came. She had hung around in the background of the establishment and then had, by a series of clever moves, become Helen's personal maid. Not, I was sure, out of any desire to serve her. But to learn from her, and to remain in the central core of the situation which was developing, in order to be there when something broke.

This was really the only thing that was absolutely clear. There had, from the beginning, been no possibility of a status quo. Something was cooking. The two girls had evolved a conversational pattern, because it is evidently necessary for women to talk even if they do not like each other and cannot understand each other. They each talked their own language softly chattering and nodding their heads and waving their hands like two birds perched on a twig. Marie-Thérèse stole things from Helen and copied her. Helen watched and hoped to learn some ancient African secret from the black girl whose silky flesh both fascinated and repulsed her.

Henry was the most interesting person of the lot of us. The most complex, being a man, and an extraordinary man at that, both physically and mentally.

Women, whatever anyone said of them, whatever their race, were essentially simple. Their mystery was this simplicity which was so great that no man could quite credit it. They were like hens, like birds, continually seeking by one means or another to collect the materials of a nest, and having made it of the most expensive materials available, they wanted to lay an egg in it. The fundamental difference in women was that some, most in fact, preferred other women and children to men. Those were, in principle, what were called good women. The others who liked men were, again in principle, bad women. But all women were collectors, hoarders of valuable and shiny things. If such things — jewels, furs, baubles — were not available, other things would do. Their hands had to be filled before they gave their bodies. And black or white, the Colonel's lady or Judy O'Grady, the principle remained constant.

But Henry was something else. He had power, brains. In some ways he was almost a genius. Utterly unscrupulous, utterly cold, driven by forces beyond my comprehension he was, I was sure, under his false good fellowship, his high ringing laugh that left his blue eyes as cold as ice, a man driven by devils, a man possessed. A man who tortured not only other people but himself, impaling himself on the pin of his own curiosity, making himself suffer; forever creating new and horrible situations to see what he would do, to see how he would wriggle out of the trap he had set to catch himself. He was a born leader. But born out of his time. Too late or too soon. He might once have been a notable pirate, or a leader of free companies. Later, today, he might have been a dictator or a gangster, mixed up with every racket from narcotics to women.

In a way I liked and admired him. In another way I feared and loathed him. But this was more or less true of the lot of them. I both liked and hated Henry. I was so near to loving Helen, only a hairsbreadth away from it, that I almost hated her for what she would do to me in what I knew was just a matter of time. And Marie-Thérèse I needed. She was the safety valve that protected me from Helen, but I hated her as the instrument of my degradation.

The obvious course was to get to hell out of it. But that was impossible. Where would I get another job even if Henry would let me go? Besides, I was in too deep. I was part of the pattern. Already woven into it and beyond extraction.

I pulled up the truck in the partial shade of a big thorn. I put a cushion near the trunk and sat down to have my lunch. I had my shotgun on the ground beside me. I had a bottle of warm beer, some bread and a tin of corned beef. What more could a man want? Lots maybe, but when you're young and hungry a meal is a meal. There was a certain interest in this brand of corned beef. The can had a label with a Negro's head on it and there had been some difficulty in explaining to our simple savages that this was not a picture of the product.

For the moment I was happy. My worries were fifty miles behind me. I was alone in Africa. In this wonderful unchanged continent. Hanging like an angel on a wire in a pantomime. As far as Africa was concerned, I had just about as much reality. I was just as helpless as she was. If the technicians did not get her down she'd hang there till she died, hang like a live chicken suspended to die of starvation, and dry into a soiled feathery bundle, in a witch doctor's hut. My protection was the truck, and my gun, my matches and the loose cartridges in my trouser pocket. Without them I should not be safe.

In Africa a man could not live without his fellows. He could not live alone. If he hunted he must have help. If he slept someone must watch. If he was sick someone must care for him. Actually, I was not quite alone. Emile, my boy, was with me. But one does not count natives, any more than one counts one's own shadow. He was a good boy who served me well. He was saving his wages to buy a wife. I was the means of his future prosperity. When he had her, and stopped working for me, I would be forgotten. I had made no dent on his personality.

He had had his food. Some manioc bread wrapped in a banana leaf tied with strips of bark, and sour milk in an old yellow gourd. Now he slept the sleep of the anaesthetized. Slept as Africans sleep. Like the dead. When I wanted him I'd have to kick him awake. Then he'd come to slowly and smile. His thick lips would open, his white teeth appear, his plum-colored mouth open in a yawn, and he'd be back from the world of dreams which he so often confused with reality. A good boy, Emile. Brave, faithful, utterly dependable. As charming and as stupid as they come, which was natural enough, considering he was only a cog from the tribal machine which a white man had borrowed for his own temporary use. In this white world in which he now moved like a zombie, Emile was happy enough. We loved each other. We thought each other mad, but interesting. I had never struck him. I had never even spoken roughly to him. I suppose I regarded him as a pet. I think he regarded me as an idiot who would unquestionably come to a bad end without his constant intervention. In those days such relationships between black and white were possible.

He lay on his belly in the shadow of a bush. He was dressed in a pair of my old khaki shorts, which were held up by a leather belt I had given to him. Fastened to it was a key to the padlock of his box, and a soft-steel trade pocket knife that he kept as sharp as a razor. His woolly head was pillowed on his arms. His feet were towards me. Their thick, pale, ash-grey soles cracked and patterned like those of an elephant.

He was near enough for me to smell him. I have never minded the smell of Africans. It is a feral smell, rather like that of the lion house at the zoo, blended with the perfume of gorse at home under a hot summer sun. Smell? After all, we all smell. We stink to the Chinese. Even our own bodies smell to us. Each part having its own odor. The armpits, the belly, the groin, the feet. Men smell of men. Women of women. These are nature's aphrodisiacs. Then, in those unsophisticated days, big business had not yet stepped in to publicize the dangers of body odor. People were not intimidated by their own sweat. They did not all deodorize themselves.

But there were other smells in the air. A sweet honey smell from the tiny white flowers of the thorn trees that were in full bloom, and a smell of putrescence, of rotten meat, that I knew came from some ants that stink of death.

Still, there was death about. There always is. That was what the gun was for. A snake, a leopard. But you couldn't shoot a mosquito, or a tick, or a tsetse, a tombo fly, a tarantula, a scorpion or a centipede. You couldn't shoot the thoughts that came into your mind, rising out of the slime of the unconscious that was so much more active here because we were nearer to the ancient savage past, and were without other distractions. Here, *yourself* was always with you. There was no escape.

It was time to go. I had come to the conclusion that there was no conclusion. I must take things as they came. Live my life as I found it. Lie on the bed I had made. But with whom and when?

"Emile!" I shouted, and prodded him with my toe. He

rolled over on his back like a big black tickled cat, smiled into my eyes, and opened his big purple mouth in a yawn. I was reassured. I had one friend. While he served me. Till he forgot me.

I said, "If there is something, you will stand by me?"

He laughed. "Me your boy," he said. "We fight. We kill." He flexed his muscles. They ran like pythons over his body, rippling the silky skin of his naked chest and belly.

The idea of fighting made him happy. That was what he was born to do. Fighting was better than bringing paraffin tins of hot water for my bath, better than making toast, which he always burned. I wanted the bread burned on the fire. It was mad to burn good bread and how could he tell how much I wanted it burned?

I slapped him on the back like a pony and said, "Fight, my boy? I hope not."

But I was happy too. There can be a relation between men, a love that surpasses the love of women. Particularly is this so between fighting men. He had seen the wound scars on my body and had asked me about them. The same tie existed between me and Henry. That was still another complication.

I pressed the self-starter. We were off again.

"And how are things with you, my friend?" Pedro said.

"They are good, senhor. Everyone is well and we have no sickness or losses with the stock."

I did not like the way he spoke, the knowing leer in his eyes, the greasy smile on his dark face.

"It will not last, monsieur," he said. "Two men and one woman, if she is beautiful, is against nature. Two women and one man is with nature." The leer spread. It ran over his face like butter melting in the sun.

The trouble was, of course, that he was right. He knew it and so did I. In his way he was wise, was Senhor Pedro. A great reader of the classics of his father's country, and also of its pornography. I doubt if anyone in Central Africa, including French Equatorial, had a finer collection of dirty pictures, although some of the best were damaged by too much fingering, and the attentions of both white ants and fish moths. Trading and women were his specialties. He was at one time, in Portugal, believed to have combined the two and spent a short period behind bars on account of it. Even today, here, he was said to be a purveyor of the more delectable sorts of black ivory and to have customers all over the Colony. But of course, in the Colony one cannot believe what one hears. One cannot even believe what one sees. Still, he was a knowledgeable man, and worth listening to, even if some of the things he said turned one's stomach.

He continued. "A beautiful woman, my boy, is like a poison. A little of it may do no harm, but a lot . . . " He was now in a confidential mood, and friendly. The wine he had drunk was working like manure in a field and would shortly produce its crop of obscenity.

But this time, at least for the moment, I was wrong.

He said, "Men and women are antagonistic. That, too, is natural, for each has what the other wants. They are like traders. Do I love my customers? Do they love me? No, but we are tied together by our desire for goods and money. There is grave danger in a woman who is too beautiful, whose flesh is too soft." (How did he know her flesh was soft?) "A man can sink in her as in a marsh, as in a bog hole, and drown in her loveliness. On the other hand, how can he choose an ugly woman and be at the same time both satisfied and safe? For if he thus satisfies his lust in porridge instead of nectar, his spirit is revolted. So there we are, us poor men — sensitive men, like you and me — caught in the trap of our desire. With a beautiful woman there is the paradox that in possessing her we are ourselves possessed. That in drinking the honey, our wings are clogged with its stickiness."

He filled up my glass with sweet, strong wine. He filled his own.

We drank in silence.

"It is always a pleasure to see you, and to hear your news. I suppose you have heard of the leopard men?" he said.

"I heard some nonsense," I said.

"Ah ha," he said. "You knew the girl at the mission died? She need not have. It was her will."

I said, "Yes. Colley told me. But that was some time ago."

"A good man, that Colley. There are not many such men who do not render their pupils pregnant. The female ones, that is. It is, of course, impossible to do that to the little black boys. But one never hears such things said of the good Colley. I hear everything here," he said. "This is a listening post in the forest and I, too, am an ancient combatant."

He always claimed this brotherhood of arms. He had served in the Portuguese Expeditionary Force in France but had spent most of his time either in Paris, or in hospital after his amorous engagements in the city of light.

"You hear everything and report nothing," I said.

"Report? Who am I to report? I am not a Belgian. I am not an official, a functionary. My God, imagine it — me a functionary! That is one thing I am not. Not constipated like those others. My bowels move very freely. After each meal," he said confidentially, "like a dog. I attribute it to eating so much palm oil and pili-pili with my food. Constipation is the cause of most disease," he said, "and, combined with chastity, may bring on almost anything, even madness."

"You do not suffer from chastity," I said.

"On the contrary," he said. "I am the enemy of chastity. It serves no purpose, and contents no one. Look at the faces of the chaste." He pulled a long face.

"Leopard men," I said, trying to dismount him from his hobby. He'd hop on again in a minute I knew, but I wanted to hear what he had to say about the leopard men. To me they were still a myth.

"Well, the rains came, did they not?"

"Of course," I said. "They always come."

"But they were very late last year?"

"Yes, they were late," I said.

"First there was the little mission girl."

I said, "Yes."

He said, "But they did not get her. The good Colley buried her in his little graveyard."

"Yes, she died," I said.

He said, "Pouf! What is death?" He waved his hand. "It is all round us. That is not what they wanted. They wanted the parts and they got them."

"Well?" I said.

He said, "There was a stranger. He passed here. He should have come back. He never returned and then there was rain. Splendid rains. Soft, continuous rains."

"Well?" I said again.

"That man was killed," he said. "His blood was taken. Parts of his body. Strong medicine was made. It is the talk of the country, and beyond it. Not only that it rained but that the rain was so beautiful, so soft, of such long duration. Such rain, they say, has not been known since the white man came."

"So?" I said.

"So," he said. "So now there is a demand for the medicine that made this so beautiful rain. More people will die. You will see. And there is something else you do not know. These parts, this blood must be taken while the victim lives to be efficacious and please the gods."

I wouldn't have put it past him to sell the medicine himself.

He said, "How long have you been here?"

"Nearly two years," I said, "but I have been in other parts."

"Other parts?" he said. "What are they unless they are in the forest? And the forest, my boy, runs from Sierra Leone to Angola and across Africa to Tanganyika. The forest is the evil corset that confines the belly of Africa. We — you and I — white men like us" (I thought he flattered himself) "will never conquer the forest or learn its mysteries. I could tell you things," he said, "the things I have seen . . . Leopard men, baboon men, crocodile men, lion men, cannibals. When I was a boy I found a hut in which human legs were being smoked like hams. I, who am still a young and virile man, have seen these things. They are not even of yesterday. Why, in the war the Belgian askaris fell upon the black German troops they killed, and ate them. Many were shot by their own officers so after that they were more careful. But I will tell you something. When a man has once eaten human flesh he gets a taste for it. Particularly here, where

there is so little meat — only game which is hard and dangerous to come by. Particularly the hands when they are
grilled upon the red-hot coals. They swell and burst. They
ooze fat. They break apart and are sucked like candy. The
hands of a man or a gorilla, the feet of an elephant — these
things are not forgotten."

I had not heard about this, and said so.

"Oh ho," he said, "what do we white men know of the
black? I trade. You raise cattle. That Colley, he saves souls
and gives aspirins to the pombé drunkards who come to him
with a headache. But Africa we cannot touch. I come
nearer because I trade. I talk their language. I sleep with
their women, not like the English in a shamefaced manner,
but normally like a human being, so they talk to me; and
their fathers and brothers talk, and I give them wine, which
is against the law. But wine is the oil of the tongue. And
they are not afraid of me. I have, a great distance back
among my illustrious ancestors, some who were not entirely
white, which they perceive." (I wondered what his mother
would think of that one.) "All the same," he said, "it is
interesting. If you do not die it is most interesting to live in
the Congo."

I said, "Men do seem to die here." I thought of several
young men too.

He said, "That is the black man's talent. Survival. That
is why he is afraid of us with our education and improve-
ments. We threaten his talent. Think," he said, "in five
hundred years there might be no great cities left with air-
planes bombing them from the sky. But in five hundred
years there will still be Africans in the forest, senhor. For in
Africa we are outside of time."

We were sitting on the stoep, or baraza, as they call it.

Behind us was the store with its piled trade goods. Canned foods, hoes, knives, three-legged iron cookpots, paints, oils, patent medicines, tobacco and cigarettes, matches, candles, cheese, lanterns, lantern glasses, spare mantles, primus stoves, adzes and bush picks, hammers, saws and other tools. Blankets, mandolins, cups, combs, straps, sweets and candies, five-pound bags of salt, whistles, chairs, earrings. And the goods that Senhor Pedro traded them for. Stinking skins tied in bundles, beeswax melted into great cones, gums and copal, native weapons and shields that would find their way into the curiosity shops of Europe, elephant tusks and hippo teeth, a few leopard and lion skins; bundles of civet and wildcat skins. They all blended into one curious smell — a composite aroma of cheese, kerosene, badly cured hides, cheap trade perfume and the smell of the African customers. It impregnated the place, and would remain there for years, even if the store were emptied. Haunting it, as if the ghosts of the goods that had passed through its doors refused to leave the premises where they had come together and consummated a marriage of Western gadgetry and African raw materials — as if things too had souls.

Behind the store were its master's living quarters, where his concubines and their varicolored children swarmed, humming like bees. Between the two, the front shop and storeroom, and the disreputable back, which he not inaccurately, but unknowingly, described as the backside of the store, came a sort of long parlor where he had his office and in which, like a spider he spun the webs of his commercial intrigues. It was here that, as a white man, he entertained European visitors who came by road or river.

In front of us as we sat on our deck chairs, the Lukuquila

rolled in slow, sullen, leaden flood towards the Congo, towards the sea, towards eternity. There was a certain interest
in thinking of it, in thinking of each drop of water as sentient.
Its one desire to join the sea, as a Christian longs for heaven.
Fighting its way towards it, its wish to cease being a drop, as
it had been when it fell from the skies. Wanting company,
wanting wholeness, wanting majesty, wanting to join the
other waters where, with them, it could show its power over
men by drowning them, by mashing them against the rocks.
Where it could fight against the earth itself by battering its
ramparts, on the riverbanks, or tearing at its sandy beaches
where it fringed the sea. Without water we could not live.
That is more particularly apparent in Africa than elsewhere,
but still I had come to hate water. Hate the torrential show-
ers, hate the spongy marshes where death lurked in the man-
groves, hate the sullen rivers which, without warning, showed
the teeth of their sudden rapids. There was always too much
or too little water so you were constantly aware of it either
making dams to conserve it or repairing the damage after
floods.

Beyond the river was the forest. The deep forest of the
primeval past, created by God and then forgotten by Him.

A pirogue flashed by downstream, in the center of the
river. The sun caught the paddles of the naked men who
drove it through the water. They shone like steel, as white
as spears, tinged with the blood of the fading light. Up-
stream they kept near the shore where the current was less
strong. But going down they rode its gallop with wild cries,
like a man urging on a horse. Fragile as straws in the
current, these great hollowed trees of wa-wa wood were
manoeuvred as delicately as feathers by their crews, who

had traveled these waters from father to son for a thousand years. These men were fishermen, water men. It was said that farther up some had web feet. This I did not believe, but if I stayed here long enough I would believe that also.

Sometimes a hippo bull upset a canoe, sometimes one charged it, biting it in half with his great tushes. Sometimes, particularly if it was a small one manned by a woman alone, a crocodile would lever itself out of the water onto the bows and overturn it. Often, women washing on the bank were taken. Dragged down by the hand that held the laundry, or swept in by the saurian's tail, which, in deep water, pirouetted like a dancer, standing almost on its head to deal her a back breaking blow. The crocodile cannot bite portions off the body like a lion, so it leaves its prey to rot into softness, fastened beneath the roots of some tree that overhangs the water. Once, some of the native tribes did that too. Cannibals, remarkable for the horrible effluvia of their bodies, who ate human bodies raw, and putrid from prolonged immersion.

Sometimes I felt that this habit epitomized the white man's position in Africa. That he was submerged in its immensity, that he was rotting slowly and would eventually be devoured. Yet, he could never get away. If he went away he returned. Africa held him in its grip, in its current, in the slow tide of its rhythm that got into his blood, changing its tempo as surely as it was changed by malaria, thinning it down, exciting it with fantastic nostalgias when he thought he had escaped.

But I was in a bad mood, depressed and tired, caught like a nut in the crackers of the present. I could see no future, no tomorrow. It was impossible not to think of all this here, on the Beach. Beach. A wholesome word, recalling sand castles and children playing, and young mothers with sweet, milky breasts. But here meaning the waterside, anywhere. Meaning the traders' jetty, meaning even the street of shops and stores. Even the trading center in the interior where there was no water — another word for Main Street. Meaning originally the Beach from which the slaves had once been loaded into the waiting ships that lay at anchor in the roads.

As if he knew my mood, Pedro remained silent. Then we had dinner. More red sweet wine, small fresh-water shrimps, and one of Pedro's laxative palm-oil stews with pili-pili, fu-fu of mashed manioc, rice, and manioc leaves served green, like spinach. Canned peaches with canned cream. Coffee followed and Portuguese brandy. Then, inevitably, came the dirty pictures. They were always served with the brandy. He even had some fresh ones, more revolting than the old. A new man, he said, a veritable genius, had taken them in Lisbon.

An evening with Senhor Pedro da Costa was quite an education. The morning after was always a headache. But he was a good host and with my morning coffee came a Portuguese version of a prairie oyster — a mixture of raw eggs, Worcestershire sauce, brandy, Fernet Branca and quinine. It is hard to imagine a more horrible or a more efficacious mixture.

Then I got down to business and loaded up our stores. Cattle feed, flour, bacon, dried fish from the Canary Islands, and smoked caterpillars for the boys, some axe heads and bush picks, a roll of game riems — thongs cut from the skins of the wildebeest — two five-gallon drums of dip and various other stores and groceries. Tea, coffee, a bag of sugar, toilet paper, canned goods — corned beef, pork and beans, canned peas and asparagus — two bags of stock salt, a small five-pound bag of table salt. Stock medicines and remedies, candles, cigarettes, rolls of boys' tobacco, snuff, all the usual mixture of necessities and luxuries that are needed on a farm in the bush.

Then there was the mail. The business mail addressed to the manager, some personal letters for Henry. One for me from my long-suffering mother. Nothing for Helen — there never was anything for her. I picked out three cloths for Marie-Thérèse. The latest and most fashionable designs for, strange as it may seem, the ladies of Africa are very fashion conscious, and will no more wear an old design than the women of London or New York would wear clothes that they consider out of date. One was dark red with a design of harps on it. Another was olive-green ornamented with red butterflies, and the third was yellow blotched with black leopard spots. God knows why I bought it. I suppose unconsciously I must have been thinking of the leopard men.

8 The Road

The road back was exactly the same as the road to the Beach. By this I mean there were no distinguishing features, except the position of the sun, to indicate in which direction I was facing. A patch of bush, a tree, a forest section are not like a village, a farmhouse or a church at home, which look different from different angles.

A man ought to know whether he is coming or going. I would later as the sun went down, because then I would be driving into it instead of having it behind me. I do not know if I noticed this then, or much later when I thought about such things, and my life, which at that time had a kind of terrifying treadmill sameness, an endless circling about an emotional center that was like the vortex of a maelstrom. I knew it was there but kept trying to look away. Trying to pretend it did not exist.

When we reached the tree where I had lunched on my way out I pulled up and lunched again. It looked just as it had looked before. I even found the empty corned beef can, which showed that no one had passed this way. The natives like cans. They fit twisted wire handles to them and use them as cups. I again sat with my back to the tree. Again Emile lay on his belly under the bush. The picture was repeated in its entirety except that the truck faced west instead of east.

I took the mail out of the bag and examined it again. I would read my letter in a minute. I was in no hurry. My mother's letters were never enjoyable. She loved me too much. She thought too much of me. To her I could do no wrong. It would have been much better if she had disliked me, much easier if she had been ashamed of me. Much better if there had been no news of the house or garden, of how she was looking forward to my coming back. I had no intention of coming back. This time I had gone for good. I had been absorbed into the great family of familyless men. I fitted in nowhere through some defect of my character, some weakness. The war had unsettled me, but I do not think I would ever have been settled. At one time I had wanted to run away to sea and would have done so if I had not found out in time that I was a bad sailor. I was evidently, by nature, a rolling stone. Moss had no appeal for me.

I opened the letter. It was like all the others. Filled with love, understanding, gentleness, hope, patience, beauty that gripped my heart and made my belly contract. If I could have, I would have gone back. If I could have, I would have changed my nature. But it was too late now. One

day I would return but only when I had achieved success.
I suppose I was rather like a girl who has gone to Hollywood and won't come back until she has made good. Like
the girl I had been going to show them. So far I hadn't.
I had merely failed in a rather unspectacular way in new
and distant places. If the company gave me a station of
my own, a ranch or a plantation, that would be different.
Then I'd have something to show. Now, as an assistant
manager, what had I? I was not even a good enough liar
to be able to weave a convincing story about my fine future.

I put the letter in my pocket. I was not looking forward
to answering it.

I looked at Henry's personal mail. There were six letters.
Three at least were from women from the writing. Two
from the same woman were written in a large, bold, sloping
hand on pale, mauve, perfumed paper. I sniffed the en-
velope. He must have had a good leave, I thought. I
wondered what she was like. What they had done together.
Made love? Almost certainly. What had he told her? Did
she know about Helen? Did Helen know about her? I
looked at the postmark — London, Sloane Square. Well,
it was none of my business but one couldn't help thinking
about such things. There was so little to think about.

Three natives came along the road towards me. One of
them was carrying something. They stopped by Emile.
He woke up. They greeted me. I replied.

"Where are you going?" I asked. I knew of course. They
were going to the Beach. To the store. They were standing
by the truck on the far side of it. I strolled over. They had
put a small buck on the ground by the front wheel. It
looked up at me out of great brown eyes. It was not tied.

Why did it not run away? I touched it. It flinched from my hand but did not get up. I put my hand under it. Its legs were broken. I should have guessed at once, and would have, had my mind not been occupied with Henry's mail. They were taking it to Pedro. They had trapped it and then broken its legs so that it would live but could not escape. Had it been dead it would have gone bad before they got to the store. The Africans are very logical. Very practical. Pedro never hunted. He could not leave the store. But he liked a change from the local goats and sheep and always bought what game they brought him.

I said, "What do you want for it?"

They said, "A hundred francs."

I offered them ten, and they took it, laughing.

I told Emile to kill it. It gave a frightened kind of bleat as he bent back its head and severed its throat with his small, sharp knife. It lay on its side, its smashed legs twisted grotesquely, like a broken toy on the bare red ground of the road. Its blood ran out, dark and glutinous.

Emile dragged it to the truck. Henry would be pleased. He liked venison. At least its pain and terror were over now. The natives were arguing and laughing. When they had gone I asked Emile what they had said. I could not speak their local dialect, only the vehicular language.

Emile laughed. "Monsieur," he said, "they do not know whether to spend the money on beer or women." To that end the small buck's agony.

We set off again. I called that particular tree the halfway house. I always tried to stop there. Now it held another memory. I wondered what my mother would have thought. I wondered if I would have bothered to do anything about it if I had not just had a letter from her. A year ago I certainly would have bought the buck, or shot it without buying it. But I had hardened, changed. It was rather strange to think of the letter. That it was my mother's hand stretched out over the sea that had made me act as I had. It was as if she, acting through Emile, had slit its soft brown throat. There was now a string that tied the dead buck bobbing about at the back of the truck to my mother in her garden at home.

Only here does one get such fancies, only here do sentiment and brutality, another word for reality, weave themselves into such patterns.

When I got back nothing was changed. Henry took his mail. Helen looked at him reading it with wide, grey, wondering eyes. I knew she was thinking: Will I ever get a letter again? But who was there to write to her? The casual lovers who had used her? Her dance-hall friends? Who was there?

I said, "I got a letter, Helen." And something impelled me to give it to her. Now my mother was also tied, on this same day, to a little dance-hall tart, the wife of my friend (was he my friend?) with whom I hoped to commit adultery. Did I? Would I? I knew I would when the time came. The moment of opportunity. She knew it too, and now avoided me as much as I avoided her. But we were fastened together by the elastic of our desire. We could pull away. Stretch it. But the instant we stopped pulling we snapped back closer than ever.

"How lucky you are!" she said.

"Lucky?"

"To have a mother." Tears flooded her eyes. But she

did not cry. I think she was cried out. They came the way water comes into a hole when you strike water, welling into it, finding its level and remaining there.

"She must be very nice," Helen said.

"I'd like you to meet her," I said. Would I? Was that what I wanted? For the moment I did. My mother would take her as she would have taken the buck. As, when I was a child, she had taken birds with broken wings and abandoned baby hares. And now, through my mother's letter, I had bound Helen to her. Another curious triangle, Mother, the buck and Helen. Had I wanted this?

"I brought back a buck, Henry," I said. I did not tell him the story.

"Good!" he said.

I did not tell him I had bought it. It was not worth while. I'd never see the ten francs again. Not that I cared. But it would have been the same if it had been a hundred, or a thousand. I heard someone shouting.

"What's that?" I asked.

"A bloody nigger," he said. "I caught him yesterday. He had killed a calf." Henry's face was suffused with blood, his small eyes blazed. Someone had touched his cattle. His love. My God, how he loved the stock! And the love was reciprocated, which was even odder. He could do anything with animals, although he did not work them much. He was too heavy to ride and left most of the stock work to me.

"I gave him a hiding," he said, "and shut him up in the store."

"He yelled all night," Helen said.

"Bastard!" Henry said.

I knew where he had put him. A small building with

barred windows and a heavy door that we sometimes used as a store, sometimes as a sick ward if one of the boys needed special attention, and sometimes as a prison if we had to hold someone till we could get them to the Chef de District.

"I'll take him in tomorrow," Henry said. "You had the truck today."

I said nothing.

"I hope he doesn't go on screaming," Helen said, putting her hands to her ears as if to cut off the noise.

Henry would be away two days. We would be alone. The tempo was increasing, the vortex approaching. I could feel it dragging — pulling at me. I got myself a whiskey and soda.

I said, "Have one, Helen?"

"Yes, please," she said. She had begun drinking now. I poured one out for her and another for Henry. He had given up gin in Africa unless he could get Plymouth.

We said nothing. The imprisoned man continued to yell like a maniac. Sometimes he screamed like a chimp, then he seemed to sob and gave a sort of choking cry. Henry got up and put on the gramophone. "Let him yell," he said.

Dinner was not a cheerful meal. Anything, even Pedro's vomit-making pornography, would have been an improvement on this music with its background of screaming. I could see that Helen was on the verge of hysteria.

Henry was smiling to himself. "That'll teach them," he said. "Teach them to touch my calves. Once that kind of thing begins . . ."

"They're meat hungry," I said. "Meat mad."

"Let them hunt," he said.

Let them eat cake, I thought. It was no use saying it. Helen would have said: "Where can they buy cake?" I could not have stood it.

We all drank rather more than usual but in spite of it I slept badly. I woke several times. The yelling was really maddening. The man must be a maniac, stir crazy. There were Africans who could not stand being shut up. It sent them mad with claustrophobia. Some races even died if shut up for more than a few days. I got up early and thought I'd go and look at the prisoner. He had quieted down now. There hadn't been a sound for some time. I remembered waking, hearing nothing and thinking he must have exhausted himself and be asleep.

But it wasn't quite like that. When I got up to the store-room I saw the boys collected near it. Half a dozen of them. They looked excited, uneasy. They moved their feet up and down, restless as horses. When they saw me they came towards me. The capita, the boss boy, said: "Come monsieur!" He took my arm, something he had never done before.

When we got near he pointed to the ground. It wasn't very light yet. I went close. He pulled me back. I looked more carefully. There was a thin black line that led from the bush to the store hut. It might have been drawn with a paint brush. It ended at the door.

"My God!" I said. "Ants. Driver ants."

"Fourmis," he said.

And the man? What chance would a man have? It was getting light fast now. I went nearer to the black line. It was about three inches wide. A solid stream of ants was moving towards the store. It was guarded by the soldiers.

They were much bigger than the others, with enormous mandibles. They stood two deep, one on top of the other on the outside, like troops lining a street while the procession between them went on. How many were there? Millions, hundreds of millions. Nothing could resist them. I thought of the old story of the boy who cried "Wolf." If he had not yelled at the beginning of his incarceration some notice might have been taken of him when he screamed in his torment. He did not know the story, I thought.

We went up to the room and looked in at the window. There was no man. Only a skeleton. It was black with ants. It looked as if the bones wore a black, moving suit. They crawled into the eyes and nose sockets, into the cavity of the sagging jaws, in between the teeth and then on, over the remains and out of the window on the other side. They had finished him. He was now only an obstruction to be crossed. A bridge of bone in their line of march. They looked like a black, extra wide typewriter ribbon being pulled slowly through the tiny building. This was something that Helen must not know. I could see the marks of his fingers where he had torn at the hard clay of the whitewashed wall. There were great red streaks of blood where he had grabbed at it with broken nails.

And there was nothing we could do. Only wait till it was ended, till the last ant had gone. They had their line of march; to disturb them would only change it. It would not stop them.

But of course it could not be kept from Helen. The place was in an uproar, everything disorganized. The line of march must not be broken. As long as they were not disturbed they would go on and on and on until the great trek ended, till the rearguard reached what was now the front, till the last ant came and went.

But even if it had been possible I do not think Henry would have tried to protect his wife from this awful knowledge. To him it was nothing. It was just one of those things. One more event like any other. I think he was amused at her horror.

As for me, I felt very little personally. Only for her. The *I*, that would once have been horrified, was lost in my pain for Helen. If it had not been for her I do not think I should have felt much more than annoyance at the trouble that would be caused by such a happening.

It went on night and day for three days. The line of march was followed by birds, black drongo shrikes with forked tails, blue bee-eaters, small red hawks who struck like Cossacks, swiftly rising and falling lest they themselves become the prey, on the small animals and insects — the crickets and grasshoppers, spiders, mice and snakes, which fled from the ants. Hovering, fluttering, diving, screaming, the birds rejoiced in the feast.

To the ants who had consumed him, two miles away in the forest now, the dead man had been nothing. Just meat. That he had moved was immaterial. For once on him they moved with him. Like children on an enormous floating boat of candy. They continued to eat as he scrabbled at the walls, as he hung, desperate, screaming from the cross-beams of the hut, as he rolled upon the floor. A few hundred were squashed but what were they among hundreds of millions? Everything is a matter of proportion. The ants were invincible. Lions and leopards, elephants and snakes all fled from them. And insects, the praying mantis — himself a terrible fellow — and the tarantula, they took and left empty, leaving only their outer shells, their skeletons in which they differed from man and other animals because it was external. But what is the difference to the ant whether they consume the inside or the out? Consumption is their life, their destiny. Terror is only a by-product. Somewhere in the depths, below the ground, their great maggot mother had spawned endlessly, eaten endlessly, loved occasionally, if fertilization is love. Then the moment came. The instant God had chosen. And the myriads went forth to consume. Fire was the only thing that could stop them. Ash, its residue, the only thing they feared. A fire would stop them. Ash deflect them. In a sense they were purpose itself, and purposeless; blind destroyers driven by hunger.

The dead African had not disappeared. He was still there. His bones were in a bag in the truck that Henry was driving to the Chef de District like a hearse. His flesh and blood and nerves moved, rustling on a million legs through the grass and fallen leaves of the forest. The African was gone but he had not disappeared.

9 The Leopard Cloth

The death of the African had had no effect on the boys or Marie-Thérèse except to give them a subject for conversation. Most of them would have liked to see him die. It would have been amusing. The division between amusement and horror for them was less wide than a human hair. Besides, it was not so long ago that their fathers had pegged men out on disturbed antheaps, or had buried them up to their chests in the vicinity of a nest after having cut off their eyelids and lips and smeared them with honey. Driver ants. Well, everyone knew about them. Everything that could run ran from them. Things that could not run, like a baby left unattended, were consumed.

What had happened was no surprise. It left them unmoved. But Marie-Thérèse, or Maigunda as her African relatives called her, took the opportunity of Henry's absence at the Chef de District's headquarters to visit her village. She was loath to go while he was there in case he wanted her back or decided to break open her room and throw out her things. But with him away she had come to a decision at last.

Her mind, part black, part white, had for a long time been divided between acceptance and revolt, between doing nothing and doing something. The tendency of the African is to do nothing, to wait for Africa, for the forces that govern his life — the forest and the river, and their gods — to operate, and then suddenly, unable to stand inaction any longer, to do something, anything. To make a sacrifice, to kill. But not necessarily his enemy. His mind is occupied with his enemy but anyone else in his path will do. Their killing is symbolic. This was her African nature but it was overlaid with her father's blood, with the remnants of her European instruction at the convent, with reason. She felt the moment had come to act. This was her opportunity.

She did her hair with care, parting its fuzziness. She rubbed her body with the salad oil she got from the cook, put on her best rolled gold earrings and her new leopard-spotted pagne.

In her heart there was a song and she stepped lightly on her bare feet down the path. First over the open veld, then through the savannah scrub, and finally into the darkness of the forest where the path was soft with the humus of fallen leaves, and so to the village. It was dusk when she got there. She would spend the night.

It seemed to her that she was looked at coldly. That the children ran from her, that the men turned their backs on her shining beauty, that the women left their cooking fires and went into their huts. She felt alone in the village. I have grown away from them, she thought. I am evolved. They are like animals. Like beasts. They are filled with envy. She went to her mother's hut. It was like a big inverted bird's nest, blackened with the smoke of the fires that killed the mosquitoes, some of the other less hardy parasites, and preserved the thatch by coating it with the tar of the woodsmoke.

Hardly had she squatted on her heels by the iron pot that was simmering in the red wood coals, when a young man came in.

"You must come, Maigunda," he said.

"I must?" she said. "Who says so?"

"The old one."

"Ah," she said. "I was coming to see him anyway. I will come later."

"Now," he said.

"All right, now." She got up with one movement, uncoiling her body like a snake. She saw her mother's eyes shining like black agates in the tiny flame glow of the fire. She had not spoken. Neither when she came in nor when she left. She wondered why. The old one. The ancient one. The wise one. The doctor wanted her.

She followed her guide through the deserted village. To its outskirts where there was a compound of several huts linked together with hanging mats, and walls made of stone and clay. As she stepped through the narrow gateway she was seized on either side by two men, masked and dressed in suits of woven raffia. Over their eyes they wore tubes of wood that ended in white painted disks. They projected from their masks as the eyes of a snail project from its head. There was a ruff of raffia round their necks. A short, stiff ballet skirt of the same material went round their waists. They wore little iron ball rattles on their ankles. These were the doctor's assistants. Those who fetched and held the boys when they were circumcised, who bound the victim of the sacrifice while their master wielded the knife. They were the ones who ran through the village at night, beating the women and children. The men who whirled the bull roarers. Terrifying men, who, when they put on their strange ceremonial suits, ceased to be men and became something more. Something in between men and god and beasts. Even if the village people knew the identity of the masked man, as soon as he was dressed he lost his individuality. He became someone else, something else — the spirit of the forest, something no longer familiar or even human. These uniforms, like union suits, were ancient, handed down among the servants of the cult. They were sacred, masculine. Few women, if any, had ever seen them so closely. For women ran from these wielders of rods and power. Part of their function was to terrify women, to keep them subject to men. Few had seen them dressed in their finery. Few who had had lived.

What had she done? She had wanted to see the doctor. To get something from him. She had money to pay for it stuck in her loincloth. The notes were soft, with the sweat of fear.

Someone invisible to her threw wood onto the fire. It burned up brightly. She could see the compound clearly. The walls of the huts were hung with sacred objects — horned buck skulls, the skulls of goats, of crocodiles. Long dangling python skins, the skins of smaller snakes, the carapaces of tortoises, the skeleton of a big fish, dried white egrets dangling from extended wings. A festooned string of gin bottles strung by their necks caught up the light of the leaping fire. A human skull rested like an ornamental vase on a thick post in the center of the compound, staring at her with black, empty eyes.

Then he came. The old one. He, too, was dressed in raffia but his skirt was longer. The ruff round his neck stuck out more stiffly. His mask, with its tubular white painted eyes was circular like those of the others, but it was surrounded by a great, round frill — a sort of sun of tall feathers. He advanced towards her with a series of running jumps. He looked enormous. His hands were raised above his head. They hardly showed in the darkness so that the pale woven arms of his suit seemed handless. More assistants came out of the darkness, surrounding her. She was no longer held, but pinned by her fear to the spot on which she stood. A bull roarer was whirling. At its sound every hut in the village would be closed as if against lions, hyenas, leopards, all the prowlers of the night were less feared. Food left cooking outside would burn in its pots. The fires would die as if killed by the sound, for no one would tend them.

Then he spoke.

"You have dared, Maigunda, you have dared to don the coat of the sacred one, the spotted one. That is for men alone," he shouted. "Strip her! Strip this female thing, strip her to nakedness! Strip her so she will see that she is not a man! That she is only a woman. A womb that walks. A place in which men may plant their seed. What is woman," he shouted in a cracked voice, "but a thing, a carrier and a nourisher of seed? A field to be ploughed by men, to be hoed by men, to be cultivated by them."

Her fine pagne was torn from her. She revolved as they pulled it off for it was rolled round her. She stood naked in her loincloth.

"The loincloth, too," he said.

"The loincloth," the others shouted. "The loincloth!"

Now she stood naked. A black Eve surrounded by devils, by satyrs, by gods. She folded her hands in front of her in an act of modesty.

"Beat her!" the old man said.

They beat her with white, newly peeled wands. As they beat her she ran. She leaped the fire. She tried to hide in the darkest corners of the compound. She crouched like a whipped dog, howling with terror, her head bowed, her breasts against her thighs. But they beat her up. They beat her down again. There was nowhere they did not beat her. Her back, her buttocks, her legs, her belly, her thighs, her very breasts. Nothing was sacred to them. No part of her. Then, at an order, they stopped.

"Now you can go," he said. "Go back to your white masters — yellow whore that you are!"

One of the men picked up the notes that had fallen on the ground.

"What is this?" he asked.

"It was for you," she sobbed. "I came to buy medicine. I have something else too." She looked for her loincloth and found it. From a little pocket sewn into it she took a small packet, wrapped in a rag, and opened it. "Here are some finger and toenails, some hair, some blood." The hair was long and golden in the lantern light. The nails red slivers like the tongues of snakes.

"So you want death. You want me to make death?" The old man laughed. It was a strange, cackling sound in the silence of the night, something that resembled the first part of a cock's crow and ended in a hyena's moaning laugh.

"Aai. I am the master of death, for death is easier to give than life, though I can give that too. Come," he said.

She tried to put on her loincloth. It was snatched away. He had her money, the little rag and its contents, in his hand. She followed him like a beaten dog; as naked as a dog without its collar. In the hut he lit a stable lantern with a match and hung it from one of the crossbeams. The weak light dimmed by the smoky glass illuminated his store of medicines. They were stored in parcels of raw hide, in horns, in boxes, in white man's bottles, in gourds; there were the mangy skins of every species of animal, tails of the elephant, the giraffe and the sable. There were blown birds' eggs in strings, great ostrich eggs, chunks of stone, distorted roots, bundles of leaves and herbs. Hanging from a peg was a leopard skin, its headskin shaped as a mask, its forelegs sewn together into gloves.

"Sit," he said. He pointed to a stool carved in the form of a coiled snake. "So you wish to kill. Aai, I can kill for you. Slowly or fast, painlessly or with pain. I am the master of many deaths."

She said, "You will make a medicine? A strong one?"

"I have one here." He gave her a little horn stoppered with a plug of beeswax. "You will give it when the moon is full. And I, on that night, will make medicine here with what you have brought me." He gave his curious hyena laugh.

"Now go," he said, "and be silent. You have seen nothing, no one. Should you say anything, you will die." He pulled off his mask and threw the leopard skin over his back. His face was hidden. She saw his eyes in the leopard's face. His arms were the forelegs of a leopard. He drew an iron rod out of a gourd. But it was not a rod. Its end was divided into sharp, shining spikes. He drove it whistling through the air with a downward stroke. "So women die," he said.

"Aniotos," she breathed. "Then it is true?"

"What is true?" he said.

"Leopard men." She knew it was true. She could not imagine why she had spoken.

"There are only leopards, woman. The killers of the forest. The spotted ones. Go and forget." He pointed with the spiked claws to the door. His eyes glared at her through the eyeholes of the skin. In the yellow gloom of the lantern light he had ceased to be a man. He was a leopard.

She crept out and ran. She ran naked through the forest, along the path over the veld pursued by phantoms. By trees which seemed to be dressed in raffia garments, as they stretched out their hands towards her, touching her with the fingers of their branches. Once she screamed in terror. In her hand was grasped the medicine horn.

It was like that — hot, wet with sweat and trembling that she ran into my arms. I was on the path beyond the garden when I heard someone running towards me. I stepped into the bamboos. As she came abreast of me I caught her. I had recognized her by the perfume, Helen's, that still clung to her, a strange yet familiar odor of scent that was mixed with her black sweat. She gasped and then clung to me. A naked woman, aroused with beating, and fear.

I had been driven out of the house by the devils of the

night. The air of the thick, soft, warm night and the thoughts that were a torment to me. Thoughts of Helen alone in the house, with Henry away, and waiting for me. Because she was waiting, I could not go. This was the one thing I wanted to avoid. But it was sending me mad. I put my foot between Marie-Thérèse's legs and threw her down. For an instant she resisted. Fighting me with straining muscles. Then, in the darkness of the night we mated like animals. Furiously, brutally. She giving herself in wild abandon, as if she hoped to rid herself of her memory of the last few hours by putting this act between the past and the future. As if she could pare the past away with the knife of her lust. I was no better. I took in hatred what I could have had in love from Helen. Took what had driven me out into the night. In one dark instant we had gone back fifty thousand years. We were not man and woman but primitive elements. The male and female caught in their male and femaleness. Caught as a tree trunk is caught and throttled by a liana.

Then I felt her searching the ground with her hand.

"What have you lost?" I asked.

"My horn," she said.

I found it. "What's in it?" I said. I knew where it came from. I guessed. "Poison?" I asked.

"Of course," she spat.

"For Henry?" I said.

"For her," she said. "For her. She has spoiled everything."

"You shall not have it," I said.

She flung herself at me. I knocked her down. She fastened her teeth into my calf. I forced open her jaws by pressing my fingers on her cheeks so that they were bruised against her teeth. She let go and I hit her with my open hand, knocking her flat again.

"Fool!" I said. "Did you think you would not be caught?"

She got up and slunk off in the darkness. I was left with the little horn in my hand. I was ashamed, but not entirely. I have often thought of it since. Then, in that moment, I had been more man, more male than ever before or since in my life. There had been no thought, no inhibition. Only action. The action of the bull, the stallion, the ram. I had known the primitive rut of the past. So must our ancestors have acted before they became preoccupied with thoughts of sex and death. These are our great preoccupations. The focus of our unconscious thoughts. The amazement that we should be involuntarily aroused. The terror that our life should ever end. The animals are happier knowing nothing of such things. The cattle that stand lowing and thrusting their horns above a beast that has been killed are not aware that they must one day die. The bull smelling the cow with bared teeth and drawn back lips is unaware that in mounting her he is performing his part in the miracle of procreation.

For once I had been at one with nature. At one with all male living things that were not men. And I had saved Helen from a poisoner. There was no need for regret. The milk of disgrace was spilled.

In our world, the civilized world of today, it was rape. In the world into which we had dropped, the hole in time through which we had fallen, it was nature in violent operation. The primal act in its most savage context. Had we been four-footed beasts it could not have happened. Marie-Thérèse had paid the price of her humanity. She had been taken by force, as women, since they first stood erect on two legs, had been taken.

There had been no real resistance. Little more than a reflex at being suddenly grasped. Perhaps it was all natural, which was why so few men who attacked women were hurt by them. After all, a woman's fingernails are dangerous weapons. Eyes could be gouged out, lips or noses bitten off. Yet only once in my life have I seen a man with a scratched face.

Trembling and shivering in her room, Marie-Thérèse felt nothing. Only the aches of her beating, the pulse of her wild blood. She was conscious of the great truth that women were doomed to be mastered by men, as no mare, or bitch, as no baboon is mastered. Woman's only defense of poison, against superior strength, had been taken from her. But she was in no way dissatisfied. Nearer to the earth than a man, she felt that something had been done, something that corresponded to the onslaught of the savage rain upon the soft, tilled soil. How the rain beat upon it, falling upon it in masculine, savage sheets; flattening it with gusts of wind that drove the squalls down as if with passion! How the soil was flattened, like a woman beneath the rain! How it responded! Hers was the wisdom of the ancient people, the Africans to whom all increase was one.

With the white part of her mind she knew that there would be regrets, that there would be presents. With that knowledge, with the happiness of blackmailed gifts to come, with her body now relaxed, satiated with the events of the night, she slept, dreamlessly as a child.

10 *The Bull*

The last thing Henry said before he left in the truck to see
the Chef de District and explain what had happened was:
"Don't forget the bull." As if I was likely to.

I said, "I'll do him tomorrow."

There was nothing much to it, although he was a big
chap. Three years old. And I'd have to arrange to get
some other cattle into the kraal with him. I had twenty
oxen sent up and got out the burdizzos. We used them
for castrating rather than a knife. They are large, heavily
nickel-plated pinchers that work like bolt cutters with a
kind of double-jointed knee action that gives them their
leverage. They are remarkably practical, easy to use, and
function by so compressing the nerves and arteries that
feed the testicles, without cutting the scrotum, that they
atrophy. I tested them with a bit of string that I folded

into a piece of brown paper. I closed the pinchers on it and when I opened it the string was cut and the paper intact. In practice they do not cut the cords which are much stronger than string. They merely press them flat.

There was no great need to try them out, but it was a precaution that I always took in case someone had been fooling about with them. The boys, if they got hold of them, were quite capable of using them as pliers or wire cutters. The great advantage of this instrument is the fact that the operation is quick, almost painless, and completely bloodless. There is no wound so there is no danger of infection or fly blowing. Dr. Burdizzo, the Italian veterinarian, by inventing them performed a great service to the stockmen of the world, and the stock — the male part of it, at any rate.

The bull was standing in the kraal with the two young oxen who had kept him company for the three months we had been trying to build him up. He seemed to have put on no weight but his two young friends were as fat as butter. I told the boys to bring in the oxen. They drove them in and began to move them round. The bull joined them, easily distinguishable by his greater size, the hump on his back, and the disdainful look in his eyes. He was still a bull.

I looped one of the new game riems over the end of a long bamboo and went in to the cattle. The boys speeded them up a little. I ran beside the bull, the riem trailing behind me like a snake with four boys following it. I held my bamboo against the bull's near hind leg. When he put his foot in the loop, I struck, laying back on the riem. The boys picked up the slack. We had him. His hind leg was pulled out almost straight behind him but he dragged us. If he managed to turn he'd charge and we'd have to bolt for the rails. Four other boys now popped another riem over his horns. Now he was held at both ends and we eased him towards a heavy post that was set in concrete in the center of the kraal. The boys at his head took a couple of turns round the double ring of No. 8 wire, which lay on the ground by the stump, surrounding it. They brought the bull's head up to the wire ring and made him fast. I threw another riem over his back and caught the ring that lay on his off side, poking it towards me with a stick, and put my end through it. I now had a running noose round his belly. As I pulled it tight, he sank onto his knees and then went over with a bellow of fury. As he fell, the boys turned his head upwards so that his horns were on the ground. The other boys pulled his tail between his legs and up over his thigh, holding it there while they lashed his hind legs together and then pulled them out. Now it was all over bar the shouting.

I knelt by his belly with the pinchers and was about to put them on the nearest cord — it takes two applications, one for each — when I heard the riem snap. As I put my arm up to protect my eyes, the bull brought both his legs back together and kicked. He cut open my forearm and sent me sprawling. Or at least that is what I was told had happened. As far as I knew I had been about to cut him one minute and the next — it was actually about fifteen minutes later — I was lying on my bed with Helen beside me. My arm was bandaged. There was a basin of bloody and dirty water on the floor beside her. What a fool I was. Fancy being kicked like that. I must have been careless. Not looked at the riem for faults. Of course after last night I was not at my best.

Helen had a half-glass of brandy in her hand. It was my toothbrush glass. The bottle was on the table. She was looking at me queerly. As if I was a child, tenderly. Her lips, soft, moist and shiny, were parted, her mouth partly open. I stared into it as if it were a flower. Into its dark pink depths petaled with white teeth. She pushed the glass into my face, spilling some of the brandy over me. I took a gulp and sat up.

"You're better," she said, with a kind of sigh. The glass fell from her hand and rolled on the floor. It did not break. I remember thinking what a good thing it did not break, as if it would have mattered.

"You're better," she said again.

Of course I am, I thought. What a silly thing to say.

Then she said, "I thought you were dead."

"That bloody bull," I said.

Two tears hung poised in the corners of her eyes. I wished they would run down her face and not stay there in that silly way. I sat up. Her face was close to mine. Very close. I saw myself reflected in her eyes as if they were mirrors. I saw the room behind us. Everything was distorted, the reflection convex, as it is in those mirrors one sometimes finds in an amusement park, or as a room is reflected if you stare into the round belly of a silver teapot. I had often done this as a child when my mother had a party and used her best tea service. It was fascinating. Helen's eyes grew larger. I felt her breath on my face. Then I had her in my arms. Now I've done it, I thought. The inevitable had happened, or was about to happen. The whole thing was unpremeditated, a single complete experience that continued without pause. I do not know how she got on to the bed. There was no resistance, no acquiescence. The arm does not acquiesce when it raises food to the mouth in a natural reflex of hunger. There was just strange fulfillment, a release. It was as if, after a dark night, the sun had risen. And how dark the last night had been. The trigger, I thought. It had only needed this to set off the already explosive charge.

She got up and smoothed her frock. "I'll make some tea," she said. "That's what you want now, a nice cup of tea and an aspirin." She walked slowly out of the room.

Tea and an aspirin. The universal remedies of the British middle class for all events that are paranormal — remedies equally for death or passion. How banal. How odd. In half an hour I had passed from the danger of death into the sin of adultery. I felt remarkably well after it. Even faintly amused. It had all been so simple, but I was in love. And I was loved. I had seen it in her eyes. Something irrevocable had taken place. It was strange to love someone so simple, so innocent. For whatever her experiences had been they had not touched her. She was like a child. A half-educated child at that. I doubted if she had ever read a book after she left school. "Answers" and "Tit Bits" were about her mark. Her cup of tea, I thought with a smile. How natural she was! How lacking in coquetry, in the airs and graces of the ordinary woman! She had never required them.

I got up, combed my hair with my left hand and wiped my face with my washrag. My shoulder was very stiff. I did not feel any pain in my arm. I decided it was still too bruised. Then I went into the other room.

Helen was sitting at the table like a hostess with a pot of tea in front of her. There was a bottle of aspirins on the tray. She smiled at me. "I made it myself," she said, as if making tea was an accomplishment. "The water was really boiling and I warmed the pot."

It certainly tasted better than the tea the boys made.

Emile came in. "Monsieur is O.K.?" he said.

"I'm O.K." I said. It always made me laugh to hear him say O.K. He had just picked up the expression.

"It was a sad moment, monsieur, when they brought you in. For my part I thought you croaked."

"Takes more than a bull to kill me," I said. Then I said, "And the bull?"

"O.K." he said. "The boys do it. They always want to try. Bull ox now. He run with others. He eating, monsieur. He not know he bull no more." He went into roars of laughter. "Ha ha," he said. "A man he know, a bull he not know."

"That's enough, Emile," I said. "I'll call you when I want you."

"O.K. monsieur." He was still chuckling.

Man. Bull. A strange affair this business of virility, of masculinity.

Helen's eyes were downcast. Her long lashes lay curved upwards on her cheeks. I knew she was thinking that one did not talk about these things. Not in Golders Green.

Butter would not have melted in her mouth. She was always like that after it happened, and it happened often. She came to me eager as a doe to a stag. Walking daintily, prettily, and when it was over she was calm again, suburban, a different woman — composed, still, sitting with her hands folded in her lap, back in the daydream world from which I had aroused her. It was as if now and again she put on her hat, left the house, and went into a walled garden to pick the flowers of love. Now she was arranging them in the vase of her memory. When they were withered she would go out to pick some more.

This was her strange duality. I got the idea that apart from her love for me and her satisfaction she enjoyed deceiving Henry, that she hated him, that she was paying him back in the only coin she knew for his jokes and tricks, for his insects and lizards, for other things she never told me about. That she felt in some way that he who laughs last laughs best. I got the idea that Henry had raised a devil in her, that wickedness must beget wickedness, as violence begot violence. For now I felt Henry to be wicked. Perhaps this was self-justification. Perhaps I felt that I did no wrong in taking the woman he abused. All I know is that I took her. But all this was in the future.

Now this was only the first time, and we were waiting for him to come back. He would be away for two days more. Love flowed over us, overwhelming us like a river, like a flood, like a dam that has burst. I was mad for her. We did not worry about the boys. Nothing could be kept from them anyway but no African ever tells what he has seen to a white man. Besides, they had no love for Henry and probably enjoyed seeing him cuckolded. As for Marie-Thérèse, there we just took our chance. I felt she would be afraid to tell Henry because, true or false, he would beat her.

We would sit and look at each other and then get up and

go into the bedroom. The strange thing, looking back on it now, is the lack of viciousness, even of sensuality, though it was sensual enough, God knows, in the situation. It had a kind of primal innocence. The death of the imprisoned man and the marching of the ants had affected her profoundly. Its horror, her husband's attitude to the tragedy. It was almost impossible to exaggerate the effect of such an event on a small, not very powerful feminine mind. On a girl who in her life had seen nothing except, perhaps, a motor accident, where in a busy street its results were quickly hidden and the victim whisked away by white-clad men in a clanging ambulance. This death had done something to her soul. To the roots of her personality. Till now, I do not think she had realized the insecurity of life here, or the forces arrayed against mankind on the equator. The talk of leopard men and the like had had no reality. It had been like something out of a book, a story in the *Wide World* magazine. Something that had no personal application.

She dressed my arm twice a day. It did not turn septic. She rubbed my shoulder with Eliman's embrocation. I still associate its turpentiny smell with her, with the rubbing of her soft hands. When I was with her, her eyes never left my face. I watched her dress and undress. I marveled at the beauty of her white, slim body. At the beauty of her small, firm breasts when she raised her arms to arrange her hair. At the perfection of her thighs and belly.

She was the beginning of my madness for women. Of course there had been women in my life, as they say, before. But they had been casual encounters. That had been sex, not beauty. It was now, though I did not know it then, that

I began to seek for truth and beauty in woman, seeking to possess both when I took her body in my arms. There must be other men like me who confuse a beautiful woman with God. Who worship her. Who go on and on, never seeing that the more it changes the less it changes. Beauty and truth — reality — are not things that can be held like a white rabbit in the hand. But I did not know it then, or even later.

When Henry came back I told him about the accident. All he said was that I should have looked at the riems more carefully before I used them, and then he asked about the bull. "Was he properly cut?"

I said we'd know before long because, if the operation had been a success, his testicles and scrotum would begin to atrophy.

Life settled back into its old routine on the surface, but under the skin of our open lives each of us was occupied with another secret life. And I was having trouble with Marie-Thérèse. She had been pleased with her cloths but her pleasure had not lasted. Under a white-toothed, smiling exterior, she was sullen. When I asked her why she did not wear the leopard cloth she turned a kind of ash color and would not reply. I supposed that she was jealous now that neither of us used her. I did not think she would tell Henry because she would get more out of me by remaining silent. But it was a possibility.

That was a damn bit of bad luck, Henry said. That bloody nigger getting killed like that. Not that he cared about the nigger. But the Chef had given him the rough side of his tongue. Had talked about writing to the Com-

pany. And he'd had to pay for those goats he had paid in
compensation to the man's family, to keep them quiet, out
of his own pocket. Still, it had its funny side. Us playing the
gramophone, he said. My God, that was funny in a way.
"If he hadn't yelled so much the first night . . ." he said.
"If you hadn't been away with the truck, Jim . . ." If —
what a lot of if's there were!

But the storeroom had looked pretty queer with all those
scratches on the wall where he'd tried to fight his way out.
Must have torn his fingernails off, and then he'd hung like
a bloody monkey from the rafters of the roof. Maybe he'd
set up there screaming, but they'd have followed him.
Slowly, certainly, the ribbon of ants would have climbed the
wall and gone along the beams. Patiently, more certain than
bloodhounds.

But Henry had been smart in repairing the walls and
re-whitewashing the patches. Put some dirt in the white-
wash too, so that it would not look too new and then he'd
chucked a gin bottle in the corner. Drunk. That was his
story and he'd stick to it.

And where did he get the gin, monsieur? the Chef had
asked. How do I know? Stole it, perhaps. From one of
the boys. Do you think I want things like that to happen?

Funny how little room the bones had taken up in the
sack. How clean they were. It would have been nice to
have kept the skull. It was so clean, a bit gruesome perhaps, but interesting. Quite a souvenir. In the war the
French Canadians, Indians some of them, had scalped
some of the Jerries they'd killed. He'd understood their
doing that. His mind went back to the bones. There wasn't
much to a man really. Not much that was solid. Mostly

water. That was what blood was, what a man was. Water
and twenty or so minerals — lime, phosphorus, iron, and
trace elements of various kinds.

And Helen, that silly little bitch. She was a soft one all
right. He'd thought he'd toughen her up. If I could have,
he thought, she'd have been all right. Pretty, but hard and
tough like me inside. We'd have made a pair. I could have
used her. A man could do with a pretty woman in his
life. She'd attract men that he could use. They could have
gone as far as they liked. It wouldn't matter to him
if he got results. Results were the thing. That had been
in his mind when he'd picked her out of the gutter
and made a lady of her. Women like her were rare in the
Congo. God damn it, she was unique! She should have
been the means of pulling some strings. The ranch was
only a steppingstone. He loved the stock. He loved cattle,
but he wanted success, wanted power. Later when he had
them, had money, he'd have a real ranch. His own. Then
he'd show them how to run cattle. He'd get a concession.
A big one. But what had she done? Folded up at once.
All the life had gone out of her. Sometimes he wondered
if she wasn't having an affair with Jim. Certainly her morals
wouldn't stop her. But she was too afraid of him. That was
all that kept her straight. That was all that kept anyone
straight. Fear. Fear of the policeman, of the Law. Fear of
being hurt.

By God, they'd learn who was master. He did not define
who "they" were. *Who* was everyone. He thought of the
war, of his career, of his Military Cross and bar. When he
took that machine gun post he could have taken the crew
prisoners. They'd put up their hands after the first bomb.

But he'd emptied his pistol into them. Every time a coconut. Went down like ninepins. That was what he'd enjoyed. Then there was the time he'd dropped bombs down the mouths of those deep dugouts. They'd been coming out then too. *Kamerad!* I'll kamerad them, he'd thought. And the men he'd had with him, picked men, felt as he did. Follow me through hell, he thought, just for the fun of it. That had been exciting. The noise, the cries, the smell of high explosive, of blood. The sweet smell of the rotting dead. And the larks singing in the blue summer sky while it all went on. And the poppies blooming red and the cornflowers blue. You noticed such things even when you were fighting, killing. That was what made it so wonderful. It would be nothing to kill in a slaughterhouse. But in a garden or a cornfield with singing birds.

Well, those times would not come back. But they made you tough. You learned to look after yourself. It was number one that mattered. The other people were zeros.

He got something of the same feeling when he went hunting. When he shot a buck. Heard the bullet strike flesh and bone with a thudding smack. Saw the buck check, shiver, jump and fall with twitching legs. When you went up to it you saw life leaving its eyes. That's where the life left a man or a buck. Through the eyes. They were the door. He must do some more hunting. He'd worked too hard lately. Maybe he'd take Helen with him. Do her good, damn her. Of course, it was nonsense about her and Jim. They'd be afraid. And besides Jim had taken up with Marie-Thérèse. Well, he was welcome to her. To his leavings.

A feeling of satisfaction came over him. Considering

everything he'd not done too badly, and that damn Chef de District, Monsieur Bloody Fouquet, had nothing on him. He'd sent his own explanation of "this regrettable accident" to the Company head office. " . . . these tragedies, as Monsieur the managing director must realize, being himself a colonial of much experience, were an integral part of the hard and dangerous life men had to lead in the wilder parts of the Colony. They are part of the price we must pay for progress . . ."

Oh yes, it had been a good letter and he was a valuable servant. No one knew more about running stock in the bush than he did.

He was in a good mood. A joking mood. He'd think of something good one of these days. Something really funny that would shake young Jim and put Helen in her place once and for all. As for Marie-Thérèse, the sulky black bitch, to hell with her. He supposed he should have kicked her out but it was funny to have her here with Helen. A joke. And the cream of it was her being taken on by Helen as a maid. He thought of those black hands on her white body. And he'd had them both and could again any time he felt like it. It was a pity that the best jokes could not be shared. Of course Jim knew it, but somehow he didn't seem to appreciate it. That was one thing he had against Jim. No sense of humor. He had no time for a man who could not laugh.

Sometimes as I rode over the veld I thought about mankind. How terrible it was. Men had only succeeded in surviving because of their ferocity. No other animal was as savage. No other mammal that I knew of ate its own species, unless it was starving. In no other species did the male kill the female, and in no other species did females kill their young or the males. In no other did the males fight without the incentive of sexual desire. In no other was the female taken unwillingly.

And this was our million-year heredity against which was tossed, like a feather ball, the religion of Christ. I had got over the killing and warrior phase which all young men seem to go through, duplicating social history in their lives as the human foetus duplicated the evolution of man in its mother's womb.

I realized I was lucky. Luckier than Henry, who was still tied to the pleasures of the chase and death by the umbilical cord of his war experience. He had enjoyed the war. Being utterly without fear and as contemptuous of pain as if he did not believe in it, at least for himself. It was a point of view I could appreciate as one appreciates the reasons for which a child pulls the wings off a fly or the legs off a grass-hopper. They do not think of the grasshopper. Do not see themselves as living in the same world, impelled by the same forces, created by the same God. Thus to see the fly crawl, the grasshopper helpless, presents to them a spectacle that is interesting, even amusing. That is the point of view of the savage. It accounted for Henry's jokes, as he called them. On this level he was blind, blinkered, by his own lack of feeling.

There were great objections to being a man. It was very hard to believe I was constructed in God's image. Some-thing must be wrong with either me or God. There was good in me and bad, but the balance changed continuously. How beautiful my hopes, my dreams, that were all cen-

tered on Helen. How curiously they ended. The end was
the same as those I had experienced with Marie-Thérèse,
only with her there had been neither hope nor dream. So
the dream ended in fornication or adultery, and of the two
the adultery, which had the dreams, was considered worse,
as sins go, than the fornication. But who had set up this
scale of values? Who was the judge?

I was not equipped to deal with these questions of morality, of ethics and metaphysics, but I had to. They were
forced upon me by circumstances, by time, by opportunity
— the trinity which produces both sin and virtue. The
situation must be there before a man can be either good or
bad. But who sends the occasion? God? Fate? I knew
Colley's answer — "That these things were sent to test us."
But why try a man so hard? Why drive him with his life
force till he must turn and fight like a cornered rat? Why
imbue him with the powers of creation and call their em-
ployment sin? No man knows the answers but every man
has been faced by the questions. Most pretended they do
not exist. Most are ostriches burying their heads in the
sands of evasion. But here there was no evasion. Given
the forces, the X and Y of the equation, there was no alter-
native.

What would you have done if you were a young man
in his full strength, utterly alone? If you were a young
woman lost in a world to which you were a stranger, one in
which you had only one thing to sell, one thing to trade for
security? Or to offer in love? There can be no judgment
from the suburbs.

Even now looking back, I can see no answer, being the
man I was then, filled with life and confused in my search

for truth and beauty. That I was wrong, I know. That I have been wrong ever since, I know too. But to be wrong is not an answer. Everything is a matter of tensions — the way they increase, or are reduced. A man is like a pole set up and supported by ropes. As one is tightened and another slacked, so does he lean this way or that. The supports are his upbringing, his religion, his breeding, the blood in his veins, the hopes in his heart, his health, the conditions under which he has lived and those in which he finds himself. Here the knife of Africa was applied to the guys. The ropes were attacked by the sun, the pegs pulled out by the contraction of the rains, the fibres weakened by the insects which gnawed them.

Here man was subject to storms and tempests, not only to those of the savage climate, but to the psychic forces which surround him, to the parasites in his blood. To remain erect he must balance himself by spinning like a top. And finally, like a top he runs down, he totters and he falls.

For me the chips were on the green cloth now. The wheel spinning. Fate or God or nature had taken over. The relative peace of months, the routine we had built up, was shattered. What I had felt coming, as if it was a storm, was here. We were in the middle of it. All the makings had been there before. They are always there in Africa, but they had needed a catalytic. The coming of Helen had set the mechanics in motion.

Even the African might not have tried to steal the calf if he had not known that one white man was away and the other occupied with his new woman. And then, as if a magnetic field had been set up, the gods had taken a hand, piling event on to event, emotion on to emotion — the tortured buck, my mother's letter, my savage reaction towards and away from the black girl, the accident that had thrown me into Helen's arms, symbolically almost, from the loins of a bull. All had combined in a terrible concatenation — the broken lizard's tail in the red dust below the aloes, the blood-stained finger scratches on the white walls of the storeroom, Henry saying "A good thing it was not the horses." Saying it just to shock Helen. Our paying no attention, but knowing that at the first scream from the horses, ants or no ants, we would have been among them. The natives spending the buck money on beer and women, the girl that the leopard men had failed to kill, who had died just the same. The stranger who had disappeared. Pedro's dirty pictures. The white warm softness of Helen's body.

For months, for years, nothing had happened and then everything happened. I knew it was not ended yet. Henry had changed. His humor was more savage. I do not know what the Chef de District had said to him but it cannot have been pleasant. He had not believed his story of the man being dead drunk and unable to get away. But the boys would have lied. The man's family had been bribed. Compensated, Henry called it. Even murder is not a serious offense among Africans as long as the dead are paid for. They would not have had him back for the twenty goats Henry had given them to hush the matter up. But are we white men much better? I do not speak of compounding murder, but how many, even sons and daughters, would wish their fathers back after a year has passed if they have inherited his estate?

It is easy for me to say I am not like that. I am not for

I have inherited nothing. But if I had? What had I in common with my father? The generations are separate, leading different lives in different worlds. And wives? I have seen more contented widows than happy wives. For men and women are of different species, living in different and antagonistic worlds. I did not count Helen as a woman. She was a part of me. Nor the women I have loved. They have been vehicles of passion, steppingstones in my search for beauty.

In my mind was terror and lust. One moment I was being sucked down into a whirlpool of despondency, the next being swept upwards in a dust-devil of elation. My world was at once hushed and more than life size. When I took Helen I continued to see myself reflected in her eyes with the room behind me, as if I were looking into a metal teapot. In my mind as I stared I said, Teapot. Teapot. And thought, My God, is that all you can think of? Is this all you can do? This was the ultimate moment of consummation and my mind went blank and I thought of silver teapots. This what I had waited for, planned for, taken risks for, and it could not be appreciated while it went on nor remembered afterwards in its fullness. Though I continued to feel her body in the tips of my fingers when we were apart, and remembered the perfections of her body with my brain, her breasts, her loins, and thighs. Now I knew the intolerable ache of beauty, for only thus could man possess it, and then only for an instant because his desire for beauty, for perfection, was lost in the act of an animal. So much was desired, there were so many dreams. Here was the very rainbow beginning and ending in the belly of a woman and then all was lost, even the memory of it. These were not the gates of heaven, only the gates out of hell, out of the desire that sent men mad. The passage from the irrational into the rational, from possession into control, from hope into regret, in a process that was infinitely repeated.

It was inconceivable that so much could suddenly dissolve into so little. It was as if a diamond dropped into water became water. And the surprise of it remained. In a year, between his seasons, the rutting stag might have time to forget, to build up new hope with the velvet of his sprouting horns, but a man never forgot, and never gave up, for the devil drove him, promising that next time he would achieve his hope, next time there would be unbelievable bliss, the indescribable experience of a man who at last finds himself face to face with God.

11 The Forest

It is very difficult to describe the high forest. There are no terms. The forest is a cathedral, but the terms of architecture cannot be applied to its great pillars, its variable arches, to the green lights that pierce the stained glass of its leaves; the brown carpet of rotting vegetation that is spread down its hundred aisles. The strange choir of birds and monkeys which suddenly give praise or scream in terror. The organ music of the branches rustling in the wind.

Is it God or the devil who lives here? Or both? The forest is a place of awe, of terror. Out of it rise the emergents — this is the botanist's term for the occasional giants that dominate the lesser trees. The dictators of this vegetal world, which may run two hundred feet before forking into branches. Below them come the ordinary trees, flat as a table top, matted with intertwining limbs, with lianas; jealous of each other, holding each other back till a giant falls, when they race upwards to take his place.

There were no gorillas here. There are none south of the Congo, but there were chimps, and monkeys and birds. Grey parrots illuminated with scarlet. Big hawks, eagles that made their platform nests in the high trees. Leopards lay at rest on the branches, sleeping with their dewclaws engaged in the bark. There were elephants, and small buck, no bigger than hares, bush cow — the red forest buffalo, and snakes, looped forest pythons beautifully marked with geometric patterns, and others more ordinary-looking and more dangerous.

I brought Helen to the high forest once. She said she would like to see it and Henry had offered no objection, but when we were in it it terrified her.

The forest when it is damaged is swift to come back. It waits for man, it pauses, and then returns. Round every tiny clearing it stands ready, poised. Its trees rise straight towards the sky, a living wall. Its borders are lashed together with ropes of lianas, decorated with blood-red flowering shrubs, with enormous leaves, with scented lilies, with the torn flags of the wild bananas.

Inside, in the depths, great trees grow and die, torn down by age, and the weight of the creepers that have climbed them and which, when they fall, suspend them till they disintegrate within their basket cradle. Sometimes they are not strong enough. Sometimes the monster is too big and it crashes to the ground, but often it remains standing, dying like an ancient warrior on its rotting feet.

The clearings are brilliant, shimmering with butterflies.

But the day is often silent. Only at night does the forest truly wake.

The paths are tunnels through the oppressive forest, in which one can hardly stand erect. The land is seldom flat, but rolls and climbs, falling at times into deep ravines where the going is easier as the leaves and branches grow higher, seeking the distant light. Everything is wet and verdant. The patches of moss are a livid, almost yellow green. The big flat leaves of the bulbous plants are dark, shining with moisture, and appear to be varnished, like green patent leather. Fallen, moss-clothed trees, eaten away by termites, fall to pieces at a touch, and swarm with bluish scorpions. There are clumps of ferns, giant palms, wild bananas, great tree buttresses coated with velvet moss on which ferns, lichens and elephant ears have taken root. There are whole thickets of long-stemmed, broad-leaved plants. Moisture drips from everything. There are tiny rivulets running through the thick, sepia-colored humus. A water diamond trembles at the tip of every leaf.

One has the feeling of being submerged. The sky is invisible except for the twinkle of light patches that are seen through the interstices of leaves a hundred feet above one's head. The air is heavy, thick with humidity like that of a conservatory.

But if a large portion of forest is thoroughly cleared by axe and fire it will not return. Instead grass grows, sour and coarse, and a secondary growth of inferior trees, soft wooded parasoliers, and others. The noble forest has become bush, no less sinister, but without grandeur or dignity.

What terrifies one in Africa, perhaps most of all in the great forests, or on such rivers as the Congo or the Zambesi, is the impossibility of exaggeration. No word is too strong, no adjective; all are understatements. For men who use words, as we use them, have no place here. These are places of the senses alone. Their immensity is felt in the prickling of the skin over the lost muscles that govern the roots of the hair, striving to pull it erect, to bristle. The ears attempt to cock, the eyes strain as we move like hunting dogs on tiptoe, ready to jump forward in attack, or back in fear. To try to express these feelings in words that can be understood, by those who have never been here, is to fail. The most I can do is to suggest.

Helen, inarticulate as she was with her inadequate suburban vocabulary, said: "It's awful." Well, it was awful. I can use no stronger word.

There is no point here where the organic can be separated from the inorganic, where death is separate from life, for before a thing is really dead, new life has taken root upon it. Things grow upon things, parasite piles itself onto parasite. Organism onto organism. This is the very womb of the world. The air is filled with spores, with the bacteria of putrescence, each seeking a host, and each capable of pulling that host down as wolves pull down a deer. Here one gets strange growths on the skin, fungoid patches that change color day by day. Molds that are nourished by sweat.

I can no more explain the Congo to a New Yorker than I could explain Broadway to a forest-dwelling savage. I could only tell him that by night it is as bright as day. He would say: "As it is in a storm? With the light of the lightning?" And I would say: "Yes." And perhaps not be too far wrong, for what is electric light but harnessed lightning?

All the same, at this moment, I have a nostalgia for it. Or

for the man I was then — for Helen. I have often had a nostalgia for cities when I lived in Africa. And always, everywhere, a desire to be where I was not — to be two men living in two places at one time. Perhaps to be happy a man should stay rooted like a vegetable, like a cabbage till he is cut, harvested by death with his kitchen knife, and replanted in some neat cemetery, lying dead as he lived, in a street with a number over his head.

Perhaps men can be happy living like this in a little villa, with a little compound round them, with their children growing up about them as alike as peas in a pod, with a daily little coming and going, along a run, like a game trail, that they cut deeper each day of their lives till finally they cannot see over its edge, and believe it to be the very boundary of reality, of the world itself. Yet, when I see them here every day in their hundreds, in their thousands, they do not seem to be happy. They are the living dead who have left life behind them, have evaded it and all experience. Whose hands seldom touch a living thing. They do not know the feel of a horse's neck, milk of a cow's teat, the head of a dog or the back of a purring cat. The one living thing that most men touch today is a woman, and their hands are dead on her body. Cold as fish on a slab.

Perhaps happiness is just a word, an invention, like justice. To be happy there must be no thought, yet without thought there can be no conscious happiness. But if a man can only be happy when he forgets himself, that, in this age of self-consciousness, makes happiness almost impossible to achieve.

Memory is deceptive, selective as a painter, emphasizing the shadows, lighting up the highlights, changing the values as a painter changes them to flatter his sitter, for none of us wish to be seen exactly as we are. My aim is the truth, but it has been overlaid by years of deception, of lies told so often that they are believed. So I must scrape the canvas, and try to find the original beneath it, before it was embellished to satisfy my self-esteem. I have to some extent succeeded. The general pattern is there, true as life, if rather more than life size, but some detail has been lost.

For instance, I remember that day in the forest very clearly. The contrast of its darkness to Helen's fair, golden beauty. The mood in which it left us both. The peculiar brilliance of the great butterflies that fluttered like jewels in the sunlight of the clearings. There were velvety black swallowtails with electric blue markings, others with Eau de Nil green markings. And smaller scarlet butterflies and blues and great tortoise-shells like those of Europe but magnified, their colors intensified. To watch them was an experience. To see them suck the flower nectar with long curled black watchspring tongues. To see them mate in flight. To see them so alive and so fragile, dancing in the sunlight against a background of forest so dark that its green merged into black, into solidity. It was a happy day of high emotion, of fear offset by love, of a picnic, a kind of *fête champêtre*. What has struck me since again and again is the strange innocence and perfection of our passion. Perhaps because we were both so young. Perhaps because every subsequent love has carried with it the residue of those which preceded it. New knowledge, sophistication, practice which has turned a natural function into an art. Later there were no meals of love, only banquets.

The high forest lay some fifty kilometres from the ranch. There was a road of sorts that led through it. Between the forest proper and the plains which surrounded the homestead there were patches of bush which we burned down when we could, and little isolated islands of the original primeval growth which the natives had spared in their ancient war between the trees and the ground they wrested from them for their fields, because they thought them sacred. We, too, fought the forest and the bush for they were the home of the tsetse, which can neither live nor breed in sunshine. And the cattle, closely herded always, were kept away from the bush. On the plains, in the open veld, there was no danger.

We had been bitten but not badly and anyway there was no sleeping sickness here, only ngana, which kills cattle and horses. Man was safe enough. The tsetse is very resistant to slaps. They must be squashed or pulled off. I let them bite me and then killed them, as, once occupied in sucking blood, they are easy to destroy. The bite is sharp and feels like the burn of a hot match head. The flies resemble small horseflies. They are grey in color and carry their wings folded flat, close along their bodies.

Helen was very brave about being bitten and laughed at me when I swore. She was fortunate in having a skin which, though it was so white and fine-grained, was singularly resistant to bites and did not show the scars which disfigure the legs of so many people in the tropics. She was wearing a light blue cotton dress that day. It changed the color of her eyes. Though they were grey, they had some of the qualities of the sea and could look blue or green at times, according to what she wore or felt. They could darken and become desirous, slumbrous with enlarged pupils. They could pale into expressionlessness as if the life had been bled out of her. The eyes have been called the windows of the soul, but they are more than this. They are instruments of power, of energy. In the quick look between a man and woman when they first meet a message is both sent and received. Pugilists watch each other's eyes. So do animals. Every hunter knows that he must not watch his quarry. That it can feel his eyes upon it as he stalks it. He must look. Mark it and then not look again till he puts up his rifle to fire. Emotion pours out of the eyes like blood out of a wound. Goodness, vice, love, hate. The cold, shining, agate eyes of the prostitute who has known too many men are one of the visible signs of her profession. The eyes of the criminal reflect his prison experience in their flat, snake-like look.

Little things come back. The blue of her eyes and dress. The delicacy of her sunbrowned arms. The scent of her hair. The beauty of her slim bare legs as she climbed into the truck. The sense that she, all of her, in all her perfection, had been mine for a day, and the sadness that the day was over. We had shared a profound experience in which awe and love were blended unforgettably.

Going home we hardly spoke. Our mood softened the harsh world of bush and grass; the sun, collaborating with us, hung low in the sky, illuminating the world with the lilac light of early evening. Birds in pairs were flying to rest. It was spring in our hearts.

Love heightens every sense. Perhaps that is why some of us seek it, while others seek drink, its opposite. In love we find much more than ordinary life can offer. Every color is brighter, every scent more sweet, every feeling more poignant, the woman we love more beautiful. Her flesh more soft, her mouth more moist. In drink we seek oblivion — we act like children, saying, If I can't have everything, I'll have nothing. Love is the entrance to life, drink the emergency exit. We try to analyze love and then find it ends in a woman's body. So much, that ends in so little. Or goes beyond it into something much greater. Perhaps it is this greater thing that we seek. This mystery that instinctively we know only woman can solve for man. In a sense, a woman is no more love than a church is God. Both are a means to some unspecified end. But only with a woman can a man proceed, his hand in hers, towards eternity. To reach it we must have her company. To reach it she must have ours. This is where I have failed. I have been greedy, gluttonous. As woman was created out of man's rib so, to be complete, he must put her back. Into his ribs, into the frame that supports and protects his heart, his viscera. They must be of one flesh, one body, one soul.

There seem to be times when it is permitted for a man to see more clearly, to review his life in its near totality, like a film in slow motion, but shown backwards so that the results, the effects, appear before the causes. So that the quarrel, the bitter word, is spoken first, and the beautiful intimacy which was thus ended, comes later. So that we can say: What led up to that? How could it have happened? How could I have done or said such a thing? We see the money spent before it was earned. The love wasted before it was begun.

It is said that a man drowning sees his whole life pass before him. In a sense I am drowning, only more slowly than in water, in my memories as I relive them.

If, for instance, we could have known what would happen while we were away, we would not have gone, or we should have taken Bongo. But Helen was afraid he might get hurt — fall out of the car, or be bitten by a snake or taken by a leopard. Leopards love dogs.

Henry greeted us in a most friendly manner. Asked if we

had had a good time. Asked what we had seen of interest. The drinks were hospitably ready.

Then Helen called, "Bongo!"

Bongo. Bongo . . . I was surprised that he had not been there with his inarticulate howling growl of welcome when we arrived. He was a small yellow and white basenji, a native dog that Pedro da Costa had given Helen as a pup. They are interesting dogs, very courageous, wonderful hunters, but unable to bark or lift their legs like ordinary dogs. The coat is smooth, and very close like the feathers of a game cock. When hunting, the natives tie a big wooden bell about their loins. They will tackle anything — gorilla in the northern forests, bush cow, even elephant, if set at them. Helen was devoted to her dog.

Henry said, "Oh Bongo. I'm afraid I have bad news about him. I was fixing some leopard bait with strychnine and dropped a piece."

"He ate it?" Helen said. "You mean he ate it?"

"Yes," Henry said. "And then he died. I do not think he suffered much. He staggered about a bit. Then he seemed all right and then later he began shivering and twitching again. He had some spasms, and it was all over."

Helen said: "Oh Bongo, my little Bongo." And began to cry.

Henry did nothing. He just sat there staring at me as if to say: Well, you've had your fun and this is what it's cost you. Of course the interesting point was that we had had no losses recently from leopards or anything else, so there was no need to be fixing poison bait.

Helen got up and went to their room.

I did not see her till next day. She did not come in to

supper. Henry sent something to her but it came back untouched. I saw the boy carrying out the tray later in the evening. I did nothing. I was in no position to do anything. As Henry said, "These accidents happen." It was another of those little African dramas. Heartbreaking in their way.

I told Helen that I'd get her another dog. She said, "No. Not again. I won't go through that again. I must be alone. There must be nothing but me. Nothing else."

I did not realize what she meant then, but later I knew. There must be nothing outside herself that could be hurt. Herself she could withdraw, like a snail into its shell, into a numbness that was beyond hurt.

Of course Henry said he was sorry. He said it quite often so that she should not forget her dog. For weeks he would say he was sorry. Sometimes he would call him. Shout "Bongo, Bongo!" holding out a scrap of meat in his hand if we were at a meal, and then say, "Oh. Oh, I forgot." But he had not forgotten, and he did not want her to forget. He wanted the wound of her loss kept open. He wanted the loss of the dog associated with her day in the forest with me, to make her feel that she had killed her own dog.

But he did it with immense charm. It reminded me of the sweets he had bought in public, at school, for the little boys he had tortured in private. Henry ran very true to form. But after all, it was hard to blame him for his sympathy. If it was sympathy.

I felt it too. Not only for Helen, but because I had loved the dog. I have a great attachment to the animals who live in the world with us. They do not lie, steal or betray. They are without ulterior motives. Few men are as honest as dogs, few women as loving as cats. I missed Bongo's welcome when I came in, the look in his eyes, the wagging of his tail that curled like a brown corkscrew over his back. Something beautiful had gone. It left a space in my life. A line on the page of our living had been crossed out. Henry had taken our perfect day and ground it under his heel as if it had been a flower. And why not? It was his right. Helen was his wife. I was just her lover. A lover is a man with many private privileges and no public rights.

12 The Serpent

There were not many snakes on the ranch. I do not suppose we killed more than one a month near the homestead, and since Helen had been with us we had not had one in the house itself. The commonest were cobras, both the black and the yellow, and puff adders — fat, sluggish, repellent and dangerous because they lay still, till trodden on, and then struck with long, savage, fatal fangs, sometimes clinging on like bulldogs. I remember cutting one open and the young coming out of it fully formed and armed with venom. I had promised the skin to a child in Leopoldville, and seeing the moving belly after I had pulled off the skin, peeling it like a stocking from a woman's leg, I slit it open and they poured out, writhing and angry, complete replicas of their parent, miniature engines of death. The puff adder is viviparous, bringing forth its young alive instead of laying eggs.

I have often wondered about a snake's poison. Where
does it come from? Obviously from the animals they eat,
from mice, rats, birds, other snakes and lizards. But except
for the snakes, none of these animals are poisonous. But
how do trees get their poisonous berries, or bulbs their toxic
qualities? Out of the soil in which they are rooted? But
how? Would the soil show these poisons on analysis?
Where, equally, did a flower get its perfume? A bird the
color of its plumage? All must come from what they ate
and what they ate grew directly in the soil, or at one remove from it.

These were the kinds of speculation that often occupied
my mind. In cities men do not think of such things. Not
of snakes, but of, say, the origin of the gas that drives their
cars. The vast residues of organic matter that was once
alive and whose movement is now transmuted into speed
on tarmac roads. In the bush, the brousse of the Congo,
one is nearer to the origin of things. Nearer to the primary
products, to the sources, than to the finished articles. Here
the women are naked. Here the meat is alive and on the
hoof. The iron is in the spears of the indigenous inhabitants.
The wood is the growing trees, some so old that they were
saplings when Christ was crucified. Here, the world is unchanged, uncontaminated, unimproved, undeveloped. Here
man, even the savage, is an intrusion upon an older nature,
a kind of afterthought in a world where such ancient exam-
ples of creation as the elephant, the rhino and the crocodile
continue almost unchanged from the prehistoric past. Here
there is no concrete or steel.

On this particular morning I was weak with fever and
love. I had strolled into the compound, and out of it past

the aloe garden to sit on an old antheap near the great clumps of bamboo that rose like clusters of plumes out of the ground. Sometimes I met Helen here. In a low bush I saw two snakes entwined. So even snakes could love. They had my sympathy. A fellow-feeling bound us. I must have been more ill than I guessed, for it took me almost a minute to see that they were mambas. The most dangerous snakes in Africa. The only one that will attack a man without reason. And fast. As fast, it was said, as a galloping horse. There were tales of mounted men being pursued, but this I did not credit. That they were fast, I knew. I had often shot them when I was working on a sugar plantation in Mozambique. They traveled like black lightning over the tops of the bushes. It looked as if a long, thick whip thong was being dragged over them by an invisible hand.

But I was not afraid. They were fully occupied, coupled, anaesthetized by sex. One was black and one bright green, they were tied in a long metallic love knot. In the act of love that would produce eggs and then more snakes. When I left they were still there. I'd been waiting for the herd of cattle we were going to dip. When I saw their dust I moved away.

Later in the day I told Henry I had seen a couple of mambas below the compound.

He said, "And you didn't shoot them?" .

I said, "No."

He said, "Why?"

"I had not got a gun," I said.

"You could have gone back."

"I suppose I could have, but I wasn't feeling so hot." I couldn't tell him that they were making love. That I had

had a kind of sympathy for them. Even to speak of them
seemed a kind of betrayal, a breach of confidence, and I
was sorry the minute I had done it. As I say, I was in a
queer state what with one thing and another. When he
asked me where they were, I said near the aloes we had
planted. I didn't want him to go to the bamboos. We had
a kind of nest among them. Hard to find but he might have
hit on it.

Unknowingly I had sown a seed. It might have been
better if he had found our nest.

The dipping went easily. Once cattle are used to it there
is no difficulty. They are driven into the race in lots of
twenty or thirty. They plunge into the bath, swim its
length and climb out, up the ramp into the drying race and
stand there, dripping till almost dry. This is how we recover
the surplus dip which runs back into the tank. The process
is continuous. As soon as one lot is out another goes in.

While they were in the race I went over them, hand-
dressing them for ticks with a mixture of grease and Stock-
holm tar under the tails, and looking for wounds, for blind-
ness, or anything else that I could find. We checked the
switches of their tails, trimming off any hair that might have
grown. We removed all the long tail hairs, for ticks can
lodge in their roots and are kept safe, free of the arsenical
dip by the tail's natural grease. This was one of Henry's
ideas. Another was the length of the dip. The swim, and
in consequence, the immersion, was much longer than is
usually found.

The cattle were all very tame, having always been gently
handled. No boy was allowed a whip. Nor were they allowed to shout or rush the stock in any way. They were

dehorned and so made no attempt to attack each other. It is curious how cows will poke each other, seeming to seek out those of their number that are sickly or most heavily in calf.

I was feeling better now. Fever is like that. It comes and goes. I was not feeling well but I was feeling less like death. Tomorrow I would be all right. I was looking forward to tomorrow, when I should be well. And even taking pleasure in working the sleek, fat, soft-eyed cattle. This was the breeding herd. Mature, heavy cows, gravid, most of them near to calving. Old mothers. And young animals, heifers, making udders for their first lactation.

Among the cows the bulls, one to every twenty-five, moved majestically, ponderous, male, virile; they moved sleepily, as if proud of the results they had achieved. It is impossible to ignore bulls. They have always been symbolic of sex, their dangling masculinity is inescapable, with its implication of fertility. The bull, the stallion, the ram, step out of the myths of the past into the present, bringing back memories from the days when our ancestors hunted, worshipped and sacrificed them; of bull fights, of mythraic cults, of Minos. These are the strange gods that still inhabit the farmyards of today in a new commercial cult of fertility.

One does not think of these things consciously, but the thoughts are there, hidden under the stock figures, under production costs, stock losses; under feed bills and veterinary supplies. Under the strange tools of the cattle raiser — castrating instruments, branding and dehorning irons. Under the natural laws that govern increase and gestation, which are the same for a cow as a woman. And the wonder, never lost, at birth itself. At the calf — wet, newborn, with white hoofs that darken almost as you watch. At the laxative custard-like colostrum, that changes after a few days into milk for its nourishment. Wonder at nature, at God, at mystery. At the flow of blood in the veins of man and beast. In the motives and desires of each. In the similar forces that govern their behavior. The drive of mating, the mother love. The friendships and hatreds of animals. I remember thinking all this many times. I have never forgotten those thoughts. No city has been able to remove them. They have at times been covered up, lost, because of new excitements, but they have come back. They have never been totally destroyed.

It was in this mood that I returned to the homestead. Something was going on. I hurried up the steps of the stoep. Henry was standing with his thumbs hooked in his belt and a wide smile on his face.

Helen was screaming in the bedroom, "Let me out! Let me out!" The key was turned on the outside of the door.

"It's a joke," he said. "She thinks there's a snake in there. A live snake. I faked it."

Helen was hammering at the door with her fists and screaming, "Let me out! Let me out!" She sounded hysterical with fright.

Henry lit a cigarette. "Just a joke," he said. "She's so nervous of snakes, I thought this would cure her."

"Bloody silly joke," I said.

That was about all I could say. It was his wife. It was his house. I was in his employ. I thought of her sobbing against the door. On the other side of it, only about ten feet away. She beat it with her hands in a kind of tattoo.

Then she screamed and I heard her fall. She upset something as she went down. It must be the small table that stood near the door, on which she kept her magazines. I heard it crash to the floor.

"About time you had a look, Henry," I said. "I should think the joke has gone on long enough."

He got up and went towards the door.

That's when I should have killed him, when he turned. If there had been a nice crowbar on the table I might have. But you don't find crowbars on sitting room tables. I turned to look, as if God might have placed one there ready to my hand. A miracle. In my mind I felt it in my hands. I felt its weight. I felt my arm muscles raise it and bring it down. I saw Henry's head burst open beneath the blow. Now I knew what people meant when they said they saw red. At that instant I saw it. Red murder. How simple. How easy. How unbelievably pleasurable. I suddenly wanted to kill Henry more than I had ever wanted to sleep with his wife. I would enjoy it more. It would be a permanent satisfaction. Sleeping with a woman was never that. Love was never that. You were always wanting more. Waiting for the next time. Thinking of it, even before this time was finished. But murder — lovely murder, how final! How splendid! I felt queer as fury suffused me like blood. I felt hot. As if blood was running over me the way it does when you are wounded. Like hot water out of a faucet.

Then I grew cold. The way blood feels when it chills off. First it runs hot, then cold. Oh, what a lot I knew suddenly. I had seen red. Now that was over. I would never see red again, not for Henry. Now I felt cold like iron. Hard like iron. My lip had stopped trembling. I was not going to

cry. How absurd a man looks crying. I would never cry
again, because my face was hard, it was turning to stone.
The tear ducts were petrified. There were new muscles in
my jaws. I could feel them swelling. I could hear my teeth
grinding. How calm I was. I was dead. That was why.
The dead are very calm. I saw them again as I had seen
them in the war, on the Somme. The dead, hundreds of
them, calm, covered with a black fur of flies — as the
African's bones had been covered with ants.

We were about three paces from the door. All this had
happened before Henry reached it. I never moved. Somehow I knew what he would see. I knew he had killed her.
He unlocked the door, and turned the handle. It opened
only a few inches. He pushed. She must have fallen against
it, I thought. I knew she had because I had heard her.
But somehow I repeated the words again in my mind. As
if to confirm the fact. To prove how right I had been. I
felt nothing now. No pain, no sorrow, no anger.

Henry shouted, "My God!" and slammed the door.

"What is it?" I said.

"A snake," he said.

"That's what you said," I said. "A joke with a snake."

"But it's alive," he said. "It went for me. It's a mamba!"

"It must have gone for her then, I suppose," I said. My
voice was quite controlled. So this was how dead men
spoke.

"I suppose so," he said. "My God! How awful!" But
I'm not sure he thought it was awful.

He got his shotgun from the rack and put in two shells.

"I'll shoot it through the window," he said. He went out
on to the stoep.

I heard him poke the barrel through the window. The glass fell with a tinkle on the granolithic floor. Then there was a shot. I waited. There ought to be another one, just to make sure. And I certainly wasn't going to go in till he'd fired again. That would have been too easy. If he had killed one of us, why not the other, in this accidental crime of passion. This clever cuckold's revenge. He would be able to say: I was just giving it the second barrel when he came in. Oh no, it wasn't going to be like that at all. I was going to kill him. He wasn't going to kill me.

I thought how interesting hate was. How Henry and I were now tied together till death did us part, in a marriage from which there was no divorce. If I'd had the guts and the money to run off with Helen — and guts and money were curiously allied. The one was no good without the other. And it might not have lasted. But this would last. This was a sacrament.

Henry had said once, "You ought to have a hobby, Jim." That was about the time he'd begun to suspect us, I think. A way of telling me he knew. Well, I thought, I've got a hobby now. A beauty. Hate, that I can cultivate like a geranium in a pot. That I can nurse and care for till its bloom is ready to pluck.

He fired the second shot. It made a hell of a noise in the house. The whole place smelled of powder. I noticed the second shot more than the first one. I decided I had been a bit numbed then. Suffering from shock. Now I wasn't suffering from anything. I felt wonderful. So free. There was no question about what we should do now. There was no we. No worry about his hurting her. There was no her. And no waiting around for me. There was no me. There

was only this splendid hate. This hobby. And absolute freedom. Nothing mattered anymore. I could do what I liked.
I could drink myself to death. I could lie, cheat, forge, kill.
I was a purpose, not a man. The first thing I'd do was to
get Marie-Thérèse back into my room and keep her there.
That would fox him. My taking up with the nigger girl at
once. Throw him off, that would.

He was back now with the twelve-bore over his arm. He
put it down on the table. "Let's go in," he said. He led
the way.

He had blown the leg off one of the chairs when he'd
fired. It lay drunkenly on its side. There was the table
near the door she had knocked down, with the magazines
spilled like a deck of enormous cards. American magazines.
The *Post, Collier's, Vogue*. They were one of Henry's ex-
travagances. The only palliative he ever gave her loneliness.
There was a glass from the window where he'd poked his
gun through the pane. The hole in the mosquito netting
showed a ragged edge behind the glass. The mamba, cut in
half by the shot, lay in two twitching portions, like long
black pieces of rubber hose, only more metallic-looking.
The dead one that Henry had arranged coiled on the dressing table had lost its emerald-green color and had faded to
a kind of dirty olive. They were the pair that I had seen.

Helen lay crumpled on the floor in the revolting filth of
death. Her hair was spread out around her face. Her eyes
were wide open, staring. Her contracted pupils tiny, fixed
in a look of horror. Foam and saliva dribbled from her
slack, half-open mouth.

In my mind, with a different part of me — my intelligence, utterly divorced from my heart — I went over the

symptoms. If she had been killed by a viper, a puff adder for instance, there would have been patches of subcutaneous hemorrhage that would be spreading over her body.

She lay crumpled like a rag doll on the floor. I thought, How funny to have loved a doll. How funny for her to be dead, and not to feel anything. Now she was beyond pain or pleasure. She could not feel my love, she could not touch my body. Five minutes ago she could have. She must have been thinking of me, hoping I'd save her but afraid to call my name.

I thought, Of course the dead don't feel anything, about anything. So all this is nonsense. I nearly laughed. I'm getting hysterical, I thought. What struck me as so funny was that I was more dead than she, because I knew about it. Henry hardly looked at her. He was looking at the snake, the black mamba that he'd blown in half.

It was interesting to use his name to feel my lips form it. Lips that had kissed her, had kissed her body. I said, "That was a curious joke you played, Henry."

"Why?" he said.

"Because you know, and I know, that if you kill a mamba its mate will look for it."

"I didn't know that," he said.

Then he said, "I forgot."

Then he said, "I didn't know it was a mamba."

I said, "How odd. After I'd told you. She was such a nice girl."

He said, "You ought to know."

I said, "Certainly. Except for yourself I suppose no one knew her better."

He let it lie. I said no more. He was not going to get

anything out of me. I suddenly knew him so well. Better
than he knew himself. I saw he had been killing her for
months. Trying to send her off her head. Of course I'd
known it before, and so had Helen. But we had refused
to face it. There had been so many things. The scorpion in
her handkerchiefs had been dead certainly. Henry said her
dog had not suffered much when he died from eating the
poisoned leopard bait. Not quite all her birds had been
killed when the wildcat got into her aviary. And there was
no reason why pot plants should not have cutworms which
attacked their roots. No reason at all. It was just that she
wasn't lucky. After all, some people weren't lucky. And
perhaps it was that some things, like her dog, her birds,
and her plants had made her happy. Some men cannot
bear to see anything happy. It detracts from their own
importance. People can escape into happiness.

We stood looking down at her. She was very small and
slight. The mamba had probably knocked her down as he
struck. They strike with immense power. It had hit her
in the neck. Below the ear there was the discoloration of
the bite. It was turning purple now, becoming blotched
like an orchid. Her hair, that I had always said looked like
citrus honey, so thick, soft, almost white in its fairness,
looked dead. In one's hand it had flowed like honey, in a
thick soft stream. Funny that it should look dead, because
they said the hair went on growing for a long time after
death. So did the finger and toenails. I looked at her red-
painted nails, one of her little vanities. She never saw why,
even out in the bundu, one shouldn't try to look nice. "Do
you, Jimmy?" I said, "No, I don't."

What wonderful talks we had had sitting hand in hand,

tired after we had loved. How often had I kissed those fingers. How often had they caressed me. One of her sandals was off. She had beautiful feet, small and soft-boned. To hold one was like holding a flower in one's hand. How tiny the red nail of the little toe looked. It always made her squeal to have them nibbled. I knew the rest of her, all that was under that pale blue crumpled frock, better than I knew my own body, because one's own body does not interest one much.

For two pins I'd have given her a shove with my foot. This was not my Helen. This thing on the floor was nothing to me. We were dead, Helen and I. This was Henry's pigeon. "You'd better pick her up," I said. "Put her on the bed." He did not move.

"I wonder how the snake got in," I said.

"Rat hole," he said. "There are always holes. Tunnels. It got in the walls and then it dropped from the thatch."

I said, "Yes."

But I was looking for a hole at ground level. I found it in a few minutes. Henry had stooped down and was arranging her clothes. I had made love to her in that frock a week ago, and remembered her smoothing it into place. Her little cutting whip, it was made of rhino horn, was on the windowsill. I had given it to her when I taught her to ride. I pushed it through the hole in the wall. Then I went out and picked it up. There was the snake's spoor in the dust of the stoep and beyond it on the garden path. But it wasn't quite like that. It was the way I had known it would be. There was the spoor of the dead snake where Henry had dragged it to the hole. He must have enlarged the hole, pushed the dead snake in and then gone round and pulled it through from inside before arranging it so artistically on her dressing table. But I don't believe she'd even had time to see it.

It was the second spoor that interested me. That of the snake's mate which wove over it in swift loops. I could imagine it coming, furious with anger. Later, I picked it up farther down in the compound. The mamba can stand up for two-thirds of its height on its tail, and weaves there, standing much higher than a man, before it strikes. That's what she had seen when she was screaming and hammering at the door. Poor Helen. She was one of those people who seemed to be born for trouble. A born murderee. Perhaps there were people born to be murdered just as there were those born to murder. And they seemed to find each other. To be complementary and supplementary. Her beauty and her need to be protected were what had appealed to me. Her beauty and inability to protect herself were what had appealed to Henry.

The blood, almost black, still seeped from the wound. Her heart was still beating as I slipped my hand down the neck of her dress on to her soft, warm breast. How often had my hands found her breasts and held them like two small, warm throbbing birds cupped in my palms. But with snakebite the heart may go on beating for some time after breathing has stopped. I had one hand behind her shoulders. Her head sagged on the slim neck that no longer supported it. There was some vomit on her chest and the front of her dress. Some on the hairs of my forearm. She was dead, and for the first time in my arms in front of Henry. I was holding her and he was looking at us. At me with my hand on her breast. My hand that knew the whole of her, her belly, the soft warmth of her thighs. I thought: Well, he's caught us this time, my dear one. But my dear one had gone. All I had was her still-warm body, her fluttering heart. What I held was nothing, nothing to me.

"Come on," I said. "We'll get her on to the bed."

Henry helped me lift her, taking her legs above the ankles. How small and fine they were. They were the first things I had noticed about her when I had sat beside her in the truck. The first thing I had touched when I made love to her. Her body drooped in an arc between us.

"My God!" Henry said. "I didn't expect this. It was just a joke."

"A bloody silly joke," I said. "But you'll play no more on her now." In my mind I was cursing him with every obscenity.

We laid her down. I got a damp face rag and wiped her lips. I tied up her jaws with a white silk handkerchief. There were flies on her eyes when I put coins on her eyelids to hold them. I folded her hands across her breast. So she lay on the bed like a tiny crusader above his tomb. I seemed to see Bongo lying extended at her feet. Perhaps he was. Perhaps her brave little dog had rejoined her in death. That once more they were together. It's up to you now, Bongo, I thought. She has left me. Stay with her till I come. Then we left her and went for the whiskey.

We drank a bottle that night. In silence. Each busy with his own thoughts. Each alone with his memories. I do not think Henry had noticed me poke her little whip through the hole in the wall, or go out to find the spoor.

Later I made it my business to find out more about

mambas. More than I knew already, that is. They are found all over Natal in the Transvaal low Veld, Rhodesia, West, East and Central Africa. I was not the only man to see the black and green species copulating. A Mr. W. Campbell of the Natal sugar estates and Mr. Innes of the Berea had both killed them under similar circumstances. It was believed by some people that they were different species; others thought that they darkened with age if they left the trees and came to live on the ground; others that the green were females and the black males. The black mamba will attain a length of fifteen feet. The green are seldom more than eight feet long. In bush fires, they are seen gliding over the tops of the long grass and shrubs as if they had wings. They have bitten mounted men in the thigh. They can strike right and left without abating their speed. So swiftly do they travel that they seem to be bounding along with ten-foot gaps between the curves of their whiplike bodies.

They have a duplicate pair of fangs. The poison gland is behind the eyes and is connected with the fang by a tube or duct. The venom acts directly on the nervous system with all the colubrine family of snakes, and unless injected into a vein, when it is carried to the heart and causes almost instantaneous death, temporarily accelerates that organ but causes cerebral spinal paralysis. The nerve centers controlling the action of the lungs are paralyzed and breathing ceases, although the heart may continue to beat for some time. The venom contains an anti-fibrin ferment which prevents the coagulation of the blood. The pupils of the eyes contract. Saliva and foam run from the mouth. There is vomiting, and emissions of urine. There is some discoloration round the bite, but no subcutaneous hemorrhage as in viper poisoning. Of course we had a snakebite outfit, a syringe, ampoules of serum, a small scalpel, sharp knife and a tourniquet all packed in a small neat nickel case.

I became an expert on snakes. I borrowed books. I bought books. Looking back, I can now see that I was mad. Helen had sent me mad with a blend of sentiment and sensuality, but this may have been partly due to the conditions under which we lived. I do not think she, or any other woman, would have had so profound an effect on me in any other context, where there were what I have come to call alternatives. Not merely other women, but other impacts which were under my own control — a restaurant where I could get a meal, a radio I could switch on, a car in which I could drive out into the country or to the sea. Friends to whom I could talk. But again, I have to take into account my character. I had chosen this way of life. I had deliberately given up the amenities of the city. So we get back — first to the weakness of my character which had driven me into the bush. Then to Helen, who caught up in her soft hands all my hopes and aspirations, all my dreams, all the unused forces of my life, and fused them into a kind of white-hot incandescence. And then, while these feelings were at their height, she had died in a cruel joke. If it was a joke. My own feeling was then, and it has not changed, that Henry was sick of her and wanted to get rid of her. Hence the joke which he thought, if nothing more serious happened, might cause a nervous breakdown which in a country like this was almost bound to be serious. No one can afford to be sick in the Congo. Even if you were strong it required all your strength to overcome the climate and the diseases that were always waiting to attack any organism that was weakened in any way. That was the worst. At best, he hoped that what actually happened would take place. I had said I had seen a couple of mambas. The implication was that they were paired. That if one was killed the other would seek its mate. That was why he had dragged the snake through the garden, and having got me safely out of the way, pulled it through the wall into their bedroom. There had been some danger. When he shot one the other might have attacked him but he had a double-barreled shotgun and he liked to take risks. So, in a curious blend of hate and humor, he had planned this murder, covering his tracks with a clown's costume. If the snake had not come in the afternoon I think he would have found some reason for not spending the night in the house. He would have decided to go hunting with his flashlight. Thus it might have killed me too, caught, as it were, *flagrante delicto*. It was the kind of situation he enjoyed, a situation of macabre humor spiced with danger, with an end that could be only approximately gauged. With Henry something was always left to those capricious gods of chance with whom he felt himself allied.

There was no time to make a coffin. Nor had we the materials. A grave was dug. I chose the place near the aloes among the rocks that she had always loved. Henry said, "Put it wherever you think best." He was acting the part of a heartbroken man. She was wrapped in a satin bedcover and carried by Henry and me. Behind us came the only mourners. Colley in his vestments and the child, Anna, crying softly. The grave was lined with lilies that I had picked in the forest. They had begun to turn brown by the time we got there. There was a pillow for her head. It was I who jumped into the grave and took her body from Henry. I who laid her on her flowery bed. Did Henry know? Was this another of his ghastly jokes? Was this the last laugh of the man betrayed? Did he see this as a kind of final, permitted adultery, and regard her bed of flowers as symbolic? I put nothing past him, past his twisted mind.

Colley read the service beautifully, in all its melancholy. Dust to dust, and the rest of it. Then I threw a clean sheet over her and the boys shoveled the red Congo earth in on top of her. Later, pending the arrival of a stone that Henry had ordered from Leopoldville, I made a rough wooden cross.

Henry typed out a statement of what had happened for the authorities and sent me off with it.

He said, "Tell the Chef I am too broken to come . . . "

We both signed it. Colley had added his signature.

I broke the journey at the Beach and went on by pirogue. Monsieur Fouquet had gone. His replacement was a much younger man called Colbert, who was most sympathetic. Of course nothing had been said about the joke, the *farce* in French. It was simply stated that Monsieur Henry Seaman regretted to report that his wife had been bitten by a mamba that had found its way into the house and had died within ten minutes in spite of all efforts to save her.

"You had serum, monsieur?" he asked.

"Oh yes," I said.

"You injected her?" It was no use saying she had been dead when we got to her.

"Yes," I said, "but the bite was high in the neck." It was easier to put it this way. I wanted no further enquiry. For once Henry and I thought the same way about Helen.

"With a mamba it is often high," he said. "They can stand up for two-thirds of their length, as you know. Stand taller than a man."

"I know, monsieur."

"And how long was it?"

"Two metres fifty," I said. "I have the skin." I put it on the table.

He picked it up. It unrolled like a great typewriter ribbon. "What a tragedy!" he said.

"I see from the files," he continued, "that a few months ago an indigenous man was killed by driver ants on your ranch."

I said, "Yes, that was an unfortunate accident."

He said, "You have bad fortune. It makes one think . . ."

"Think what, monsieur?"

"It gives one to think," he said again. He paused. "I who speak, am not of Belgium. I am Congolais. I was born here. My father was also a functionary. So I see things in a different manner."

"What do you see?" I asked.

"You seem an intelligent young man, so I will tell you," he said. "If you repeat it, I will deny it" — he smiled — "after all we are alone and without witnesses."

He seemed to change his line and said, "My father was in these parts many years ago as a young man. He told me things . . ."

I said, "He told you?"

"He told me this was a special sacred area. At that time there was some question of its being opened up. They began a road but abandoned it on his advice. But he said to me, 'If ever it is developed, my little one, those who go there will have bad luck. Things will not go well with them.' "

"The farm has prospered," I said. "Our losses are small."

"Yours," he said. "But as an administrator I do not see things in terms of cattle, but of men. Leopard murders. The death of that man by ants. The death of Madame Seaman. I regret I never met her. I hear she was young and beautiful."

"She was beautiful," I said, "and young." How far away she seemed. "Leopard men?" I continued. "Then there is something in it?"

"There is a great deal. A lot has been going on. Proof?" He raised his hands. "Of course there is no proof. I do not think my colleague, Monsieur Fouquet, appreciated it. He is not a Colonial. Me, I feel things here." He put his hand over his heart. "You will stay the night, monsieur?" he said.

I said I would be charmed.

"It is good to see a strange face. Only tragic that it should be for such a cause."

We dined well. His conversation was most interesting. His hobby was anthropology. He showed me his collection of weapons, masks, musical instruments and artifacts. He told me stories of witch doctors, cannibals and human leopards. He talked of hunting, of the game he had shot, of serpents. Only three snakes, he said, would attack a man for no cause — the mamba in Africa, the king cobra, or hamadryad, in India and the bushmaster in South America, and some of the West Indian Islands. He told me that in the days of slavery some slave owners had imported bushmasters into Martinique to discourage the slaves from running away. He talked of the way snake poison acts. He maintained that some natives had a secret cure for snakebite.

I said, "And how does it go?"

"What go, monsieur?"

"Your work of civilization?"

"My friend," he said, "where I am there is law. There is order. It is like saying that when I switch on the light there is light. Then when I go it is switched off again." He shrugged. "But we persevere, and in time, perhaps . . ."

"In how much time?"

"A generation. Or two, or three, or fifty? Who knows? To change the African, Africa must be changed. Everything. The way of life, the conditions of life. They must have less disease — bilharzia, filaria, intestinal parasites, venereal disease. They must have protein, meat, fats. They must have education. They must work, the men I mean, not only the women. They must cease to buy their wives like working animals. They must stop drinking as they do. The women must be educated, the girls go to school. They must cease to be corrupt. Can you imagine how long it will take to change all this?"

I said I could not. How did one change the environment of a hundred million people?

The African was his interest, just as trading and pornography were the interests of Pedro da Costa, as cattle and jokes and hunting were Henry's, as my love had been mine. In Africa a man must become possessed by something or go mad.

All this is in the distant past, buried under the debris of memories even less fragrant, only now resurrected because this is the moment that the truth must be exposed, searched for, as a dog searches for a buried bone. Then, perhaps, I did not see the wood for the trees. Now, perhaps, I only see the wood and have forgotten some of the trees. It is hard, for instance, to believe that had Helen lived she would now be middle-aged, and that only death has held her memory, preserved her youth, pickling, as it were, her beauty in the brine of tragedy. Creating a myth, but the one by which I have lived. A golden fleece for which I have never ceased to search. Perhaps it was not even love that I felt for her. Perhaps it was infatuation, but the will-o'-the-wisp, the leaping marsh gas, is light, is mystery. I only know that with her I reached heights never attained before or since. What is love? How many have asked that question. How few have answered it. To begin with, each gives the other pleasure by getting pleasure; later, one's pleasure comes in giving pleasure, and finding it in the giving. But neither of these phases seemed to exist for us. We arrived suddenly at our conclusion.

Since then I have loved and been loved. Have known pleasure, and joy, and release. Have seen beauty, but never again been a part of it. What I have had since then have been reflections, mirages, which, like a man dying of thirst in the desert, I have chosen to believe were water. For a time — an hour, a day, a week or a year — they have sufficed.

Incredible as it now seems, Helen was what I sought in all these women. Gloria came nearest to her in body. But how distant she was in the spirit, in the essential that I sought. Gloria was like one of those lovely imitation roses whose falseness one cannot detect until one touches them. They have everything except the qualities of the natural rose. Its perfume, its fragility, the softness of its petals, the wonder concealed within its petaled depths are all missing.

13 The Accident

Sometimes I went into Helen's room — I still thought of it like that — when Henry had gone out in the truck with his rifle. It was safe enough even if I had been found there, because that was where he kept his safe to which I had a key, and the stock and account books to which we attended together. I would open the safe and get out some of the books or files. And then go to the cupboard.

Her clothes were still there on the hangers. She had been very careful with her clothes. Her neatness and cleanliness had been part of her charm. She always had a newness, a just-out-of-a-bandbox appearance. A fragrance like that of a flower, of a daffodil that has just burst out of its paper-like covering and turned towards the sun.

Every dress held a memory, as it had once held her body. Memories of actual love or hope of it. Under them my hands had found her body. How well I had known her with my mind, my heart — carnally, as the Bible puts it — as a man knows a woman, a lover. But more than that, in some way I had identified myself with her, become of one flesh, so that I knew what was in her mind. The thoughts she could never express with her tiny, banal vocabulary. She had never learned the grandeur of words. In her home, no songs had ever been sung. No poetry read, no pictures ever seen. When I talked of pictures, she had at first thought I meant the films. Films, movies, flicks. The soap operas of the BBC had been her escape into romance, the fragile basis of her dreams. From this sickly mess she'd reached out, seeking truth and beauty, as I sought them. It was here, in these flowery fields and mossy banks, that I had met her wide-armed. She was like a child come out of a wood into the sunlight of thought, of ideas. How often those similes occurred when I thought of her — child, sunlight, flower, fragrant.

They all came back when I looked at her empty clothes hanging in the closet like the skins of dead beasts that had once been filled with glorious life. I have seen skins like this hanging at a taxidermist's. But at the taxidermist's, the skins were waiting to be mounted. True, they would never be alive again, but they would give the illusion of life. One day, I supposed, these rags would be filled with life again. Some other woman, a black one — Marie-Thérèse, perhaps — would fill them. Henry would lump them in an armful and throw them at her, like a bone to a dog, and say: Take them.

Her perfume still remained clinging to the frocks, to the wood of the closet. A faint emanation, weakening each time

I opened the door. Fading as memory is supposed to fade, as color fades in a picture. But there was no fading of her image in my eyes. I saw her as I had always seen her, as I see her still. I saw myself reflected in her eyes when I looked into them. How many eyes have I looked into since then, seeking my image, seeking my lost one, but never have I seen it again. It was a peculiarity of hers, and hers alone, due to the way her wide grey eyes were set in their sockets, to some fantastic and beautiful accident of nature never, to my knowledge, to be again repeated.

Below her dresses were her shoes standing on their high heels like little soldiers on parade. I knew them all. There was not one that I had not taken off to kiss her feet, or hold them, soft and supple as a baby's, in my hand. Her feet were perfect, without a blemish, without a callous, apparently without a bone. She had walked eagerly in these shoes to meet me. On them she had left me. I picked up a white one. The buckskin was soft in my hand. I stroked its nap. I rubbed it up the wrong way and smoothed it down again against my cheek.

There was one pair she had never worn. The soles were virgin except for the scratches I had made with my knife to prevent her slipping on the polished floor. We kept the floor highly waxed so that a snake when it got into the house was almost helpless unless it got onto a skin or carpet. The knife was in my pocket now. How excited she had been when the parcel came. I had brought it with the mail from the Beach. She had sent to Brussels for them. Henry was prepared to spend money to dress her well. She loved shoes. She took a very small size — a three — and was proud of her feet, regarding them in a detached way as if they did not belong to her. She used to say: "I have beautiful feet, haven't I?" I would say: "You are beautiful all over." And then she'd say: "But I can't see myself all over except in a glass. Just my feet and my legs."

How true that was. A woman could only appreciate her beauty in a mirror. Her beauty was her gift to others who had the pleasure of looking at her, of watching her. A gift of God to man, rather than to the woman herself.

Henry had laughed when I'd scratched the soles of her shoes.

"You don't let her do much for herself, do you?" he had said.

I'd said: "She is not used to polished cement floors."

He'd shown no resentment. Only a mild, amused kind of curiosity that I should care whether she fell or not. He always thought someone falling was funny — an accident was always a joke to him.

Finally, and the situation repeated itself I don't know how often, when my memories became unbearable, and I'd close the closet, then I felt as if I had imprisoned her. Shut her away. But each time she lived more vividly for me. Each time some new memory, something I had forgotten with the top of my mind, came back. Some subtlety, some touch of the hand, some look when she came into the room, some promise in her eyes.

Then I would put back the books, lock the safe again and go out.

And the sun of her presence was reduced to the moon of its reflection. A pale blue light in which there was no warmth, only an ache in my arms, my loins, my belly and my hands. A tingling of my skin that cried out from every

pore, as if they were mouths, for hers, for her softness. Each
time was a new experience, each like a separate act of love,
each another page added to the book of our love, that had
not been ended with her death, that has not ended yet,
that will never end. Perhaps if it had gone on long enough
it might have ended as such things do. This I do not know.
Only that it has not ended, that the ache remains. That I
still wake in the night with her name upon my lips.

The house seemed very empty after Helen's death. The
light had gone out of it. The soul. After the first few days
Henry did not seem to be much affected. But I don't know
that anything would have affected him. For him it was just
a joke that had gone wrong. He did not seem to understand
it. That at least, is what he pretended. For me my life was
ended. I was still alive but I was a different man. I was
like a wheel wobbling on my axle. The linchpin had been
knocked out. I still revolved. I did my work. In fact I
worked harder. There was no reason to return to the house
now. No one to watch. For watching the perfection of her
movements had been one of my pleasures. Sometimes I
went down to her grave by the aloes and put flowers on it.
It entered my head to put food — dishes that she liked and
cakes, and whiskey. Like the Africans did. It was impossible to believe that she had really gone. That she would not
come back. That I would never see her come in through the
door with the sunlight in her hair. Never hear her high
heels, so unsuitable for Africa, tapping on the concrete floor.
    Then slowly an idea took form in my mind. A terrible
idea. I do not know where it came from. Does one ever?
But it came like a living thing, stalking like a tiger over the

veld of my mind. Like a leopard. I still, like so many South Africans, called them tigers. But it came slowly like a tiger, belly down, hidden behind bushes, behind clumps of grass, behind other motives, behind things which my mind said were one thing and my heart knew to be another. There had been the moment when I could have killed Henry had I had a weapon at hand. Then a kind of death with her death. Then my hatred that I had nourished but still the hatred of a man who was spiritually dead — broken by his disaster and without the energy to implement it.

Where was the new, the real beginning? When I bought the Mannlicher from Pedro da Costa, perhaps? That was a conscious act because I had said: "Will you sell it, senhor?" And I had bargained with him for it. I must not let him know that I must have it at any price. When I first picked it up it fitted my hand like a woman's breast, as naturally. The smooth nickeled action slid as smooth as woman's silk. I made him test it for me at three hundred yards. Why did I not try it myself? I forget the excuse. I bought five hundred rounds of ammunition.

But my subconscious mind must have been planning something. Saying: Do this. Don't do that. Don't try the rifle, Jim. Don't. Why not? I must have asked myself. My unconscious warned: Because you don't want him to know you're a good shot. Good? That was an understatement. A rifle had always been an extension of myself. I could not miss. I had shot at Bisley. It was owing to my score at school, we had carried off the Ashburton Shield. Because of it I had given up shooting game. It was not sport, it was murder.

The plan began to develop. To show its hand as if it were a living thing.

When I got back, Henry said: "Why, I thought you'd given up shooting! You've never shot anything except a bird since you've been here."

I said, "I know. But I used to be a good shot and I'm going to try again and see what I can do."

"Try ahead," he said. He thought it a great joke. A bigger joke still when I went out day after day and brought home nothing except the story of my misses.

"I can't understand it, Henry," I used to say. "I can't understand it at all. I used to be so good." But if I missed the buck I shot at I always hit the twig or sapling beside it at which I had aimed. Or a stone beneath its legs, sending it up smashed, like an egg, into the air.

I was shooting better than I had ever shot in my life. That was all I had to do now. Just go on shooting. And wait, my secret self told me. Wait. It must not be too soon. What must not? I had no idea. Or had I?

Anyway, things went on like this for a full year. Christmas passed again. A hot, heavy, African Christmas, white in patches where the great cottonwoods blossomed their silky seeds that hung like burst powder puffs and fell softly to the ground. Henry and I drank to absent friends. There had been more of those mauve scented letters for him, so no doubt he was thinking of replacing Helen, the irreplaceable. It was to her alone I drank. My friend now forever absent. I do not believe in ghosts but I felt her presence. In the night I saw her coming into my room as she used to sometimes, for Henry slept like a log, like the dead, with a kind of gross, snorting, grampus sleep, puffing and blowing, sweating as he lay on his bed. Then she had slipped in barefooted, white as a ghost, naked under her dressing gown. She still came. Oh yes, in my sleep, and my half-sleep, I was seldom alone. It was more than memory and less than a spirit. It was an emanation, like a remembered perfume, so that I would say to myself: Yes, it was like this.

One feels this sometimes when one smells such things as violets or night-scented stocks. One remembers the way they smelled before in the long, long ago. One remembers the occasion. I remember my mother saying goodnight to me as a child when she was all dressed up with a bunch of Parma violets in her hand.

Sometimes I thought of justice. Where was the justice in the death of someone so young, so fair, so good? For there had been no wickedness in Helen, no cruelty. Her wickedness, such as it was, was an escape from Henry, a method of retaining her sanity; a reflection, as in a mirror, of his own moods that drove her to me. Justice was a man's concept and without reality. Why was it just for one man to be born rich and another poor? One clever and another a fool, one handsome and another a hunchback, one white and one black? I had no confidence in justice. The eyes that held the scales were indeed blind. Not for the cause of justice but against reason. Was it just that Henry should live and Helen die? That was the nub of it. That was the core round which my mind revolved.

Then my chance came. I did not even know then that it was my chance. Only something that I must do, in a certain way. Something I must say which would produce a certain effect.

One evening when I was out I saw the kudu. There were plenty of kudu but this was the king of them all, with long, spiral, twisted horns that reached upwards like great corkscrews opening the sky. Henry had a passion for record or near-record heads. He had splendid specimens of kudu, though none as good as this, and sable that we call swartwitpentz, and giant sable from Angola, impala, reedbuck, water buck, buffalo, bush cow, oryx from the Sudan, and bongo — oh, a fine collection. I doubt if there was a finer in the Congo, where few men will hang horns, the symbol of cuckoldry.

I told him. I told him where I had seen it. Beyond a gap, a break in the low hills. "The biggest I've ever seen," I said. He knew I had seen a lot of kudu.

"I'll go tomorrow," he said.

I said, "You'd better. I expect he'll still be there."

He had been eating beans below the trees. The curled seedpods of the thorn is one of their favorite delicacies. There were kaffir oranges there, too, another thing they love, and I had not disturbed him.

"I'm glad you didn't try for him," Henry said.

"What would have been the good?" I said. "Shooting as I do. I'd only have frightened him."

Even now I had no real idea of what I was doing. At least I do not think I had. It was as if I was being directed by some outside force, or some inner power. I only knew that I must say this and do that. That this was why I had bought the Mannlicher. Now the great moment had come. There was a beast in the forest. The bait was there. My heart beat like a bird in my breast. Beating its wings against the bars of the time that separated me from the moment that, unknowingly, or half-knowingly, I had so long desired and planned for so carefully. It was for this that I had muzzled my tongue, coated it with the honey of submission. This was the end of the dance, the last movement, the grand finale of the ballet that had begun when Helen first stepped out of the little woodburner onto the Beach. The first step had been hers, when that bare white buckskin-shod foot had touched the wooden baulks of the dock. Helen and Henry. Then I had joined the dance, circling about them. Then Marie-Thérèse had joined us in the dark background where the scenery was confused, where the spotlight never struck, but where one could feel her presence. And we, the principals, popped off the center of the stage to come to her in our turn. Each of us. Henry and I to lie with her. Helen to be dressed, to be undressed. I could see it now. Like a moving picture. Strange that I, one of the major actors, and now about to dominate the scene, had, until this moment, been so unaware of the plot.

The kudu was the bait grazing unaware, trotting magnificently through the forests, galloping with his great horns laid along his back, his chin raised as he avoided the passing branches. But couldn't all life be seen in terms of bait, of baited traps? Desire for riches, for women, for glory? What were these but bait? In a sense, to the iron filing, the magnet that drew it was bait. The field of desire was the field of magnetism. And that was more than an analogy, for certainly men and women were drawn to each other by electrical forces. They sent out waves of desire. That was what happened to us. Each of us had sent out waves, in circles, that had moved this way and that, impinging one on the other. Elsewhere, where there was more variety, there would have been other forces that might have neutralized them. But here there was nothing. Nothing to distract any of us. I now saw the thing, and it was a thing, a situation that had lived, objectively. Saw myself as a cog or a flywheel turning and spinning, driving. My way was set in a groove, like a wheel on a rail. It was curiously restful. I had become a passenger. The happy passenger. The waiting was nearly over. Soon I would arrive.

Henry would arrive, too, but he did not know it. And the kudu? This time the kudu would escape. There would be an accident.

Africa is at its most beautiful in this evening light. This was the light in which Helen and I had basked as we drove home after our day in the forest. It was drink time. Sundowner time. The time when the game begins to move through the lilac light. The shadows of the trees were long. Even tussocks of grass, and quite small stones threw big shadows that were out of all proportion to their actual size. It was a lilac and pink world, shadowed with black and indigo. The yellow grass and the olive-green trees were rose-washed. There was a rush of wings as a flight of namaqua doves swept down towards the river to drink. A steenbok ram with tiny black needle horns, immense dark eyes, and ears like wings peeped over the grass and, seeing me, crept away on his hands and knees.

The late bees were still busy in the flowering thorns. Their white flowers scented the atmosphere with a perfume that reminded me of a mixture of sweet peas and lilac. The halfway house tree on the way to the Beach had smelled like this when Helen came.

I found the place I was looking for. A small flat rock outcrop almost completely surrounded by bush. I was now exactly four hundred yards from the gap in the ridge that

Henry would have to cross to get to what we called the river bush. It was beautifully illuminated. The sun was behind me. Four hundred yards. I had paced it twice. In this same light I had fired at least twenty rounds at that range and never missed. I always took out the rifle in the evening like this, and fired at something — a tree stump or a stone that I had set up, but of course I never hit that one. Oh no. There was always a second one, a secret one. I missed my target and got something near it. Not even very near. And never, since I'd had the Mannlicher, had I brought in a buck. I had never even wounded one, so that if I was watched, if one of the boys had seen me, he would only laugh. It always made Henry laugh. He was a great hunter, was Henry. And now I was taking advantage of his love of hunting to trap him. A man can always be trapped by his love, betrayed by it.

When he came, and I knew he would come, I would kill him. It was a beautiful evening for murder, for justice, for an execution. A beautiful time. Drink time, sundowner time.

When I had killed him I would go back and shout: "Boy! Boy, bring the drinks!" I would ask the boy where the Bwana was, where was monsieur. How could I know he was not there? When he did not come in we would search for him with lanterns, calling loudly. The boys would have lanterns. I would take my flashlight. What a good thing I had put in new batteries.

I was without any fear of failure, without any doubts. I was happy lying on the warm rock with my hate as if it was a woman. My hate was my love. My beautiful hate. I was waiting for the moment. My rifle cradled in my hand was

warm with the dying sunshine, shining beautifully, the polished brown wood of the stock and the small, the lovely gun-
metal-blue of the barrel — my friend. The rifle was my
little brother. The rifle was my love, my woman.

I was happy. Perhaps happier than I had ever been, even
with Helen, even when making love to her, for then a man
does not think. Then he is lost in an atavistic act of which
he retains no memory. But this I knew I would remember.
This I could savor. It was I who would pull the trigger. I
would take up the first pressure, and then squeeze softly.
I knew how it would feel on the joint of my index finger.
First pull. Then a check as the trigger meets resistance.
Then the lovely squeeze. Don't pull, squeeze. How often
had I heard that said? How often had I said it myself?

Here, there would be no repetition of the hundreds of
millions of reproductive acts that had resulted in my existence. Creating, I was an animal. Here, in killing, I was God.

Of course I was mad, and I knew it. That, too, was a
splendid feeling. It was like being drunk with one's mind
clear. It was having one's cake and eating it too. The nearest I had ever got to this feeling before was with Pernod.
Absinthe seemed to produce a parallel, though vastly inferior, state.

At that moment, while I waited for Henry to come, I
loved him for giving me the excuse and opportunity to kill
him. It had been like that with my first elephant. I had
loved him for his ivory. My excuse for causing his death.

The bird of my memory swung in slow, descending, di-
minishing spirals into the tiny past of the infant's world.
How small and warm and milky it was. A world of sensa-
tion, of unfocused eyes. For an instant I felt myself a child

again. Then slowly it grew and climbed into the future. One day the time beyond me would contract again, if I lived. For an old man's world is as small as an infant's. Like an infant in its cot, he is pinned by his infirmities. Freed so many years ago from his mother's womb, he is now returning to the darkness once again. To the cold wood of the coffin. To the lead, the bronze of the casket, the perfume of the floral tributes to his passing, mixed with the smell of his own putrescence. What he was is gone, his swiftness, his strength, his thoughts, his passions. That was the way it should be. His life a spiral swelling out into a kind of belly, like a plaited whip in his prime, and decreasing again to a pinpoint when he died. Unless he was cut off somewhere in the middle like poor Henry was going to be. But there was a certain magnificence in it. Henry would die in his power, in his glory. And I, by ending his life, was putting myself on a level with God. For only the gods can slay.

On the other hand I was performing an act of execution. An eye for an eye. A life for a life. Helen had been cut off in her prime too. Clipped like a rose from a bush, for a joke. Where was the justice in that? Justice was an illusion, a man-made word. So was freedom. A man was free only in so far as his personality permitted him to be free. His personality was the chain that held him. A man was chained, caged by his heredity and conditioning. So far you may go and no farther. This you may do. That is forbidden. The chain might be made of gold but it remained a chain. And most men were at a loss if they were freed.

He would come soon now. In my mind I saw him smaller than an ant. At three hundred yards a man of average size just about fits into the barrel of a service rifle if you take out the bolt and look through it like a telescope. That gives you an idea of size. At four hundred, Henry, who was six feet tall, would not quite fill it. There would be a little rim of space round him. The beautiful shining, silver twist of the rifling would surround him like a frame. There at the end of it would be this tiny circular picture with a miniature, ant-sized Henry in the middle of it. Henry's last picture. That was the way he would look when I put up the rifle. If I looked at him through the barrel instead of over the sights. How clearly I would see him. I had remarkable eyes. Wonderful sight, and a rifle was just a continuation of my hand. This use of tools, and artifacts that go beyond tools, is something science has not yet been able to explain. When I fired a shot it was as if I had a bullet in my hand and drove it into the target with a blow. The space between the muzzle of the rifle and the object fired at was eliminated. It did not exist.

I looked at a bluejay that had perched on the dead limb in front of me. A roller, one of the world's most beautiful birds, with an electric blue head, a pink chest, green neck and ultramarine wings and tail. The tail is forked like a swallow's. I knew as I looked at it that Henry was coming. That it would sit still till I fired. Then it would fly up, almost straight into the air before it went off with its diving flight to find a safer perch. I had not yet seen him. But I felt him coming.

I dropped my eyes from the bird and there he was strolling towards the gap. He was a poor mark really at that range in his khaki bush jacket and shorts. But not for me. He was dead already, only he didn't know it. I tried to take my mind off him because I felt he might feel me killing him.

The rifle came up softly, slowly. The bluejay never moved. How smooth, how warm, as silky as a woman, I thought again. I cuddled the butt against my cheek and snuggled down onto the rock. My feet were flat. My legs wide open, extended. There was the back sight in front of me, and the barleycorn of the foresight. I took a fine sight with that rifle.

And there was Henry with his head just visible above the foresight. The back sight framed him. I thought of the way he would look from the barrel. The way the bullet would see him. My eyes were in the bullet. My eyes, my heart, my blood. The sum total of my personality would direct it. I took the first pull. I squeezed. In the hundredth of a thousandth of a second the striker would be freed, would set off the fulminate of mercury in the cap, explode the cordite and drive the bullet towards him. Drive me forth, for I was the bullet.

The explosion came. The recoil drove into my shoulder. The rifle lived in my arms, leaping into them. The little man that was Henry threw up his hands and fell, as I had known he would. How neat. How clean. No cry. No blood. Not even a man had died. That little thing was not a man. It could not cry out or bleed. It was too far away. I ejected the spent cartridge and left it lying there. Why not? I had shot at a buck, a little steenbuck ram with horns like tiny, black needles. But as usual I had missed him and he had jumped away. Or had I imagined him? Anyway, it was drink time. Sundowner time. I would get back just before darkness fell.

I say I did not know when it began. I am wrong. It began when Helen screamed behind the door and I had first thought of murder. When I had wished for a crowbar to batter Henry into a pulp. Then I had put the thought away. It had returned as justice, as execution. That was when I had bought the Mannlicher. But I had not known it then. I had only known that I must shoot again and let no one suspect how well I shot.

It was almost dark when I got back. The house was beautifully silent. Tonight there would be no ghosts. I had a wonderful sense of completion, of accomplishment. I was relaxed. At peace. The Tilley lamps hissed pleasantly. The sitting room looked very comfortable, homelike. I called Emile.

"Where is the master?" I asked.

"The master is still out. The truck is not back," he said. "He hunt."

"Ah," I said. "Then tell the cook we will wait." He was late sometimes and I always waited.

I poured myself out a whiskey. Just two fingers, not a big one. I wound up the gramophone and put on a record. The music filled the room. I lit a cigarette and sat back. The tam-tams began as it grew dark. The fireflies lit their lamps. Night had begun. This was a memorable occasion. I would have liked to have a feast. Champagne and old brandy. We had some for special occasions. But everything must remain normal. I called Emile.

"I am going to look for the master. Something must have happened. Get out the boys and all the lanterns. Tell the Capita to come." I got my torch. "You come with me, Emile," I said.

Then I drove out the boys in groups, each with a stable lantern. They feared the night. I knew they would not search far and would end up in the village. But I was creating a pattern of anxiety. We hunted all night. I said, "The truck must have broken down."

At dawn we found him. What was left of him. The hyenas had done a good job. The vultures were picking about among the remains. They had the eyes out of his skull. The hyenas had cracked most of his bones for their marrow. The ants were busy.

It was Emile who first spotted the circling vultures. Then we found the truck. From there it had been easy for one of the trackers who had joined us to pick up the spoor. We followed the line he had taken.

This time it was Henry who went into the bag. I sent a boy back to the truck for one. There were always a few in it for the boys to sit on. There was his skull, the shivered bones, and parts of his shoes — they had been eaten too. Some rags and buttons — all that was left of his clothes — and the rifle. No shot had been fired but there was a round in the breech. The safety catch was on. There was his cigarette case dented with a bite. Almost flattened out in fact. And his hunting knife. Some scraps of paper — among them what was left of a mauve perfumed letter, damp with blood and the heavy dew.

All round him were the tracks of the hyenas, the feathers and white chalky excrement of the vultures that had quarreled over his body.

I sat and smoked with the boys round me while I waited for the bag from the truck. Then we went off. Emile carried the bag. I put it on the floor beside me while I drove back. As soon as I'd had breakfast I would take him to the Chef de District. To my friend, Colbert. I knew he would again say that this was a place of bad fortune. I would agree with him. I would write to the Company. I could do that on the way, at Pedro's, and Colbert could post it with a duplicate of his own report. I'd send a plantation runner to Colley with the news and tell him what I was doing. Say I would look him up as soon as I got back. There had been no reason for all my precautions. I had found the bullet. It was safe in my pocket. A little souvenir. I have it still. A distorted little lump of lead and nickel in the morocco box in which I keep my cuff links and oddments. Curious that I had not thought of the hyenas. But as soon as I had seen that the body was destroyed, I had told Emile to wait. I had said I wanted to approach alone. I did not want a lot of spoor round him. Then I had found the bullet flattened against the rock it had struck after passing through him.

There had been a certain perfection about the whole thing. God had been on my side. Naturally, since Satan had been on Henry's. I was nothing. Merely an instrument of the justice in which I did not believe.

I talked to the boys. "What happened do you think?"

"He must have hurt himself. A snake, perhaps? Or fallen, and then the wild beasts came."

I would suggest that to Colbert. Suggest a stroke — he was so fat. A touch of the sun — excitement — hunting. A fall, a stroke, a snake? Who could tell? I'd shrug my shoulders. My friend, *mon copain*, my comrade of so many long days and nights *dans la brousse*. My old school friend. The tragedy. First his beautiful young wife. Now the man himself. Perhaps her death had made him careless.

The day was beautiful. Not too hot, although of course it was early yet. The truck seemed to be running exceptionally well. The engine purred as if content. Henry had been hard on it, changing gear roughly and without sympathy. For after all the meshing, gears were human. Steel had feelings. Only with animals was Henry gentle, and then only when they submitted to him. First, he broke them. It was because he had not been able to break Helen, because he could not own her utterly, for although he had her terrified a small hard core remained inviolate, that he had hated her. How true it was that hate begot hate, that those who lived by the sword should perish by it. That he who sowed the wind would reap the whirlwind. How true, and how false.

The Company would expect me to run the ranch. I would do it for a year or so. Then I would go home. Now I could go. I could say: "Oh yes, I'm running a big ranch in the Congo. Twenty thousand hectares." In my mind I again heard Helen say, "And what is a hectare, Henry?" A lot of her conversation came back to me in its childish, banal simplicity. Yet how wonderful it had seemed. I wondered about an after life. Had I sent Henry to her first? Should I, later on in another life, have to kill him again? But there was no marriage or giving in marriage in heaven, they said. Since there were no bodies there could be no adultery or murder. But what after all did anyone know? Perhaps situations went on endlessly repeating themselves.

I stopped at the usual halfway house and had my usual lunch. There must be nothing different. I would like to have taken a bottle of Henry's wine. He was always very mean with it. But I didn't. I had beer and bully. I left Henry in the truck. It was interesting to think of the last

time we had been here together. When I had come to meet
him and Helen.

Pedro wanted my story. He'd heard of it already from
his boys but not the details. The drum could give no details.
I knew that Colbert would know too.

Pedro's chief interest was in Henry's effects. His rifles,
he said. "You will sell them, I suppose?"

I said, "I suppose so."

Then he said, "That was a lovely Mannlicher I sold you.
A lovely gun. Do you remember my trying it for you?"

I said, "Yes."

He said, "I suppose you never shot anything with it?"

I said, "No." My bad shooting was a joke for a hundred
miles round. "I'm a very poor shot with a rifle, but I'm all
right with a shotgun."

"How beautiful she was!" Pedro said.

I said: "Yes. She was."

"And now both are dead."

I said, "Yes."

He said, "Perhaps it is as well. There were the elements
of tragedy there. He would have been a bad man to cross."

Then we started drinking seriously.

I have an idea that he thought there was more in the
situation than met the eye. And that drink would loosen
my tongue. But I was too clever for him. I simply promised
to sell him anything of value that Henry had left. His guns,
luggage, clothes.

His smaller personal effects — watch, the crushed cigarette case, papers and so on I would send back to his parents.
I would naturally not say, Here is the cigarette case damaged by the teeth of the hyenas that ate your son. I would

have to go through everything when I got back, write to them, and to the mauve scented lady.

Next day I took Pedro's motorboat up to the Chef de District. I found him preoccupied. Even the savage-looking police askaris looked different.

The red and yellow and black flag of Belgium hung dejectedly as usual from its black and white striped barber pole. The bare parade ground remained as dusty as ever but the place had an air of waiting, of expectancy. Not for me, I hoped.

It was not for me. "So," my friend Colbert said when I went into his office. Its walls were lined with maps, with graphs and official notices.

"So," he said, "there has been another tragedy?"

I said, "Yes. You have heard?"

"Of course I have heard. Give me the details."

I gave them to him.

"Ah," he said. "Another little drama."

I said, "I have the remains in my truck for your inspection. The bones, the cigarette case, what is left of the shoes. The skull." Is it not curious how indestructible skulls are — skulls of both men and beasts.

"Mon Dieu!" he said. "Do not talk to me of skulls. Come!" he said, pushing back his chair so violently that it fell. "Come!" he repeated.

He opened the door of a small room. "Skulls," he said. "Just look at that one! The work of leopards. Except that it was found wrapped up in her own loincloth. Figure to yourself a leopard doing that. But that is what they say. A leopard did it. A forest leopard. It is enough to send a man mad."

He raised his hands to his hair, running his fingers through it.

"And here, look at this!" He pulled a crate out of a corner and tipped its contents onto the concrete floor. "Here" — he picked up a kind of poker divided at the end into three sharp prongs — "here is the instrument. Here is part of the uniform." He handed me a leopard-marked cloth.

I said, "But I know that. I bought some of that material from da Costa a year or so ago. It was the only piece."

"Yes," he said. "I have traced it to him. And you gave it to a half-caste woman. Marie-Thérèse, the mistress of the deceased."

I said, "Yes. If you want to put it that way. Is she implicated?"

"Certainly she is. She knows something. But what can I prove? You find me distracted," he continued. "Up to the neck in this affair, and then you must come with your little drama of the forest. It is sad. It is regrettable. But is Monsieur Seaman the first man to have an accident out hunting? And you — you want to show me his skull. His remains. My God! This is the country of skulls. It is not long ago that the slavers, when they made a razia, beheaded their victims and impaled their skulls on poles in the smoking villages they destroyed as a warning against resistance. Not so long ago since the doorsteps in old Calabar were made of human skulls, and the children played with them in the streets, rolling them like balls. You have read of all that. Of the ju-ju houses, of the lower jaws cut from living men because of their fetish value. It is the lower jaw that moves when men eat, when they talk. Skulls!" he almost shouted, "and you wish to present me with another!"

I said, "I only wished to have everything in order."

"Nothing can be in order here, and you will stay the night? I will give orders."

"You will make a report?" I said.

"Of course. What is another report? That is what I do. I solve no problems. I make reports."

"I would like a duplicate for the Company."

"I will give you a duplicate and then tomorrow you will take your damn skull and give it a Christian burial."

I said, "Certainly, monsieur, if that is in order."

"In order," he cried. "It is more, it is an order!" Then he apologized. "I am sorry," he said. "I regret . . ."

I said, "Never mind. I can understand what you feel."

"How can you?" he said. "You do not know. For months now it has been going on. Disappearances. One here, one there. Often a hundred miles apart but the center is at Magobo. There is a traffic in human flesh," he said, "in blood, in fat, in portions of the bodies of men. From here they go far afield. They are carried hundreds of miles into Angola, into the Sudan, into Uganda. From my district. The borfima fetish," he said, "that is not of the Congo. It is West African from Sierra Leone, but it is here, at least I think it is, here a fetish made of human flesh of the genitals and rice grains and sperm mixed with white cock's feathers and the dust taken from a market place. The whole is wrapped and sewn in human skin taken from the face of a living man and anointed with human fat." He sat with his head bowed over his desk with his hands covering his eyes.

Dinner was a depressing meal. I spent most of it consoling Monsieur Colbert, assuring him that no man could have done more, and trying to get him on to his hobbies. But the hunting stories always came back to leopards, and anthropology ended with cannibals and secret societies. Before dinner he had typed out his report and given me a copy.

In the morning I went back. Spent another night with da Costa, reassured him of my intentions about Henry's effects — like Colbert, he insisted on referring to Henry as the deceased — and then drove on to Colley's mission, where I spent another, more pleasurable, night, because of the company of my little Anna. She had become quite friendly again. I told Colley I would have everything ready for the funeral the following day.

In the morning I got up early and found the truck bound to the small trees under which I had parked it by a network of silvery spider webs that sparkled with diamond dewdrops.

"Come look, monsieur," Emile said. He was showing his splendid teeth in a smile of interest. "Come look at Monsieur Henri. The ants have found him."

And so they had. The bag in which his remains were hidden was black with ants. They had climbed up the wheels, proceeded along the axle, mounted the springs, found their way onto the bottom of the truck, which they had crossed walking upside down, finally mounting its sides and descending onto its bed.

"What shall I do, monsieur? They will bite," Emile said.

"We will do nothing," I said. "We will return home. They are occupied and will not worry us." I had other things on my mind. There must be a clearance. Henry's clothes and guns packed up for sale, an inventory made of the small articles of interest or value to be returned to his parents, the letters of sympathy to be written. His papers, many of which I thought would only upset the dear ones at home, who thought him a paragon of virtue, to be destroyed, and Helen's things, now that he was dead, to be dealt with. I would burn them. I saw them burning in my mind.

Then a new and terrible idea came to me. Perhaps Henry had loved her. Perhaps she was the only thing he had ever loved and, because of it, had feared. So he had had to humiliate her, to break her and weaken her power. Perhaps he had suffered but had shown nothing. That was his pride, in being hard, untouched by anything. Perhaps that was why he had never got rid of her clothes. Perhaps he, too, took them out and filled them with her body. The body that he knew as I did. Perhaps he too took out her shoes and held them to his face. Perhaps he saw her slender feet in them, her pretty ankles, the slim legs rising out of them. But I put the thought out of my mind. It was no use being too imaginative. Justice had been done.

Thinking this over, rereading what I have written, I can see that to some it would appear melodramatic. With the recapitulated pattern of death, of leopard men, of hyenas, and of ants, more terrible than either. But that is only because they are unaccustomed to the picture. In Africa there is no melodrama. Against that background the greatest events are minimized, reduced to their ultimate simplicity, each fitting like the parts of a puzzle into some other part. Colonial life is singularly free of all complications, of side issues. This is what gives it its dramatic, even apparently melodramatic, quality. But out there the lives of men are not important. Against those vast horizons a man is not much larger than an ant. There we all, to some extent, live as gangsters trying to rob Africa, and Africa takes her revenge. Agriculture in the tropics, on the equator, is a form of war. There are enemies on every side. From the great elephants which in a night can destroy a plantation to the small organisms that infect a man's bloodstream, and the insects that consume his crops.

It is the decorations that embellish and hide the facts of life in a civilized community which, missing in the forest, point up the starkness of the primal acts. Here they are bare, naked. As naked as a woman when she makes love. In a city it is the frills which surround and precede each act which deceive us. The soft lights of the restaurant, the swift, sleek car, the uniformed doorman, the elevator attendant. But the acts remain. The acts of love, of death, of birth can never be changed, they can only be disguised by the canopied, satin-covered bed, by the hospital nurse, by the motorized hearse. Above all by the crowds going about their own affairs, which continually surround us. There is less drama in a man run down in the heavy traffic of a street than a man dying alone in a wilderness. As a witness, your eye will be distracted by policemen, by the crowds, the people who, with morbid curiosity, hide the fallen man, by the sirens of the police cars and ambulances. In the forest or desert nothing breaks the monotony of the scene.

In the city all this is part of life. In the forest and the desert it is theatre. It is drama. The smaller the audience the greater the effect upon it. But the acts are constant. They are animal — even dying is an animal act. They make us ashamed, so we dress them up with ceremony and ritual.

This is why there must be a God. The forest god of the Africans. Colley's God. Someone has to save us from our guilt.

14 The Funeral

Henry's funeral presented no difficulties. I bought him a very fine coffin from the store at the Beach of indigenous mahogany with ornate brass handles. They were not solid, as Pedro had assured me, because when I scraped them with my knife some brass came off. But they were heavy, strong, and of good appearance. It was a coffin for a king. I did not decant his bones but left them in their bag and filled up the spaces round them with palm leaves to stop them from moving. I had thought of arranging his bones in as much order as my knowledge of anatomy and the scarcity of his remains permitted, but decided against it, since without the cushion of flesh which would have held them in place they would have rattled around in a disconcerting manner.

The grave I had dug near Helen's, and I ordered a twin headstone from the same source in Leo. I charged both the stone and the coffin to the Company, and their auditors passed the accounts.

Colley again officiated. Anna and I were the mourners with a group of curious Africans who were interested in these white man's rites. I was moved, not by the funeral, but by the memory of Helen's on this same spot. I wore a black band round my arm and afterwards told Colley and Anna, who stopped for a meal, how much my dear friend would be missed. Anna listened wide-eyed, and I do not think she believed me.

For a while I put flowers on the graves and would sit and smoke in their vicinity, thinking of them both. The beauty and the beast. How wonderful it would have been if I had killed him earlier, right at the start. But then there would have been a motive. If there are two men and one beautiful young woman, and one man is killed, the situation is classic. There had been a motive, but now it was obscure, insufficient to most people to justify killing since the cause, the prize, was dead, and so long a period of time had passed in which we had lived in apparent friendship.

There are two difficulties with murder. The concealment of the body which includes, in brackets as it were, that of the murder weapon — the gun, knife or blunt instrument of detective fiction — and the question of motive which generally lead to the perpetrator. When a man dies by violence the police always ask themselves who would gain by his death. I had gained nothing, except in becoming the manager of the ranch — a poor reason — as by Henry's death I had lost a dear friend with whom I had never quarreled, an old school fellow to whom I was attached by years of close association.

Then there had been no body. My perfect plan had, in

the end, proved, thanks to Providence and the industry of the wild beasts, quite unnecessary. Still, it had been foolproof and I had found and picked up the empty shell I had left on the flat rock as evidence of its impossibility by a man who was so poor a shot. I was without regrets, although I must say I felt a curious sense of completion, accomplishment and emptiness. I have felt something of the same emotion when I have finished a book. The project which has occupied me for so long is ended.

But Helen, and my remembered passion for her, grew in stature, became more romantic than perhaps it had ever been. It grew into the idea that has dominated my life. But men live by ideas rather than by facts. The real Helen had been canceled out by my revenge. This dream of fair women which now took its place was more solid than the granite of her headstone: Helen Katherine Weems Seaman, born Golders Green 23.7.05. Died tragically of snakebite at Lukika 20.6.25. Till the stone Henry had ordered came I'd had no idea she was called Katherine, or that her maiden name was Weems.

Henry's stone was engraved: Henry George Seaman, born Sevenoaks 15.4.1894. Died Lukika tragically while hunting 4.9.26.

I liked it. I liked the repetition of the word tragic. I liked the similarity of the two stones standing as twin monuments to two different kinds of joke — or to the joke and its answer — among the aloes and rocks of the Congo. They had a certain dignity. I wondered if anyone would ever put up a monument to me. My end seemed a long way off then.

Everyone said I was taking Henry's death very badly. Everyone being Colley, Colbert and Pedro da Costa. But

they were wrong. It was my little friend's death I was feeling now. The full reaction to my loss had been delayed. I
had been supported on the crutch of my hate for her
husband. Now that it was gone I was crippled. So both
to avert suspicion and to occupy my mind and body, I
prosecuted my affair with Marie-Thérèse with still greater
vigor and more openly. I installed her in the house. I
lavished presents upon her. She was the lovely black herring that would put anyone off the scent. How could a
man murder the husband of his mistress and then take up
with his discarded concubine? I used her again as I had
after Helen's murder, when I had proved to Henry that his
wife meant nothing to me by my actions with her. Putting
myself in the place of the curious, I asked myself this question and found no answer. No one would do it. But I had.
Once again the warm satin flesh proved my anodyne.
Drink might have brought suspicion, might have made me
garrulous, would in any case have been harder to give up,
and might have cost me my job and reputation for competence. Besides, I have never cared greatly for drink
except for wine with my meals.

My black tulip bloomed voluptuously. She swelled like
a leech with good living. She became arrogant because I
never beat her. But one only beats things one has loved or
one fears. There has to be a tie of some kind between the
man who beats and the thing that is beaten. Those whom
one despises one can only abandon or kill. When the time
came I would leave Marie-Thérèse with a few thousand
francs, her memories, and what new she had learned from me
of love. Then slowly she swelled like a great purple plum
into conspicuous pregnancy.

Well, she had always wanted a white child and I had

accorded her her ambition. I had no feeling of pride in my paternity. I have never seen why a man should be proud of doing what a bull or a dog can do, but perhaps that is because I have lived too much among animals. I was faintly amused in this new bead now forming on the endless chain of procreation. I wondered vaguely at the different hereditary instincts that would be at war with each other in this new soul now forming in her belly — at the blood of my fathers mixing with that of the assistant engineer, and the cannibal savages on the maternal side of its pedigree. I considered genetics, the laws of variation discovered by the good Abbé Mendel. I thought it strange that Condom, the discoverer of contraception or at any rate its popularizer, and Malthus should both also have been men whose profession was religion — priests, divines. I though of phallic cults. Of fertility. With this example always before my eyes what else was possible?

Finally, not wishing to bring my own bastard into the world myself, being more accustomed to the accouchement of cows, and Marie-Thérèse refusing to suffer the ministrations of the tribal midwives, I drove her to the Catholic Mission of the Sacred Heart and returned my damaged rose to the garden where her spirit had been first nourished in the Christian Faith.

I gave the Mother Superior, a charming and understanding French Canadian woman, the sum of five thousand francs, a large sum in those days, but which I could well afford, to be held for her and bid my friend goodbye.

I said, "You must forgive me if I do not come back. I have provided for you and even though I am somewhat curious to see my child it will be better if we do not meet again."

At which she turned upon me and spat. "Your child? Do you think I would bear your child? You, the Assistant Manager? This is the child of Henri that I bear under my heart."

I said: "My good woman, it is to me a matter of supreme indifference whose seed you bear in your belly. It is perfectly possible, or at least biologically possible, that the father is my friend and comrade Henry, with whom I have shared so much, but by the law of averages it is still more possible that it is mine."

With that I left her somewhat disillusioned and with lowered pride. I wanted no pale, coffee-colored bastard, but somewhat illogically I resented being betrayed.

I do not know if this is what I actually thought. It was such a long time ago. But it is what I think I thought. It is the residue of my rationalizations, the way I make sense now of what was the deepest emotion that I, as a man, could feel. My love had been killed. I had killed the killer, and now I was a father. We are always embarrassed by emotion, including our own.

The slightest error in the timing of a play can make an audience giggle and cough with embarrassment. This happens if, for one instant, the illusion that identifies them personally with the actors on the stage is lost.

I am like that now. I apply a certain wry humor to bandage wounds that will never heal. I try to laugh because I am afraid of tears when I think of my pretty Helen's bones in the red laterite of the Congo basin. Bones that were once clothed with such lovely palpitating flesh which moved with such grace that she seemed to float rather than walk.

In life there are no excuses. There are only effects and

causes. What is done, is done. It is irrevocable. No word can be withdrawn, no blow unstruck, no caress ungiven. But there are times when this seems hard to believe. When it seems impossible that the clock cannot be put back a day, or even an hour, to give us a second chance.

I think of this when I go over my life, that part of it at least, step by step, day by remembered day, and then see that, given the same days again, I would act in the same way. How could I not have loved my love? How could I not have killed my enemy, her destroyer? But it is strange that I should still ache with longing for a woman so long dead. But the ache of love seems to me stronger than any other form of regret, its acid bites more deeply into the heart. That is why it was no surprise when I thought I saw her again in the loved flesh. Unconsciously I have sought her in others, some part of her. In each, something reminded me of her. The eyes, the hair, the bow of the mouth, the fall of a wrist, the turn of an ankle, the shape of a leg, the tilt of a breast, the lovely outline of a hip; but with each I sought for more, hoped for more, watched for more, and so passed from one to another. Always thinking, She will come. One day I shall see her.

I have made money and lost it, and made it again. I have made friends and enemies. I have owned things — houses, gardens, cars, boats, horses, dogs. I have been praised and execrated. But none of it touched me deeply. Nothing has really stirred me. The hurts were irritations, the pleasures palliatives. Short oblivions I have known in the arms of a woman, on the back of a blood horse, or swimming in warm, blue water. Moments of ecstasy, of beauty that have pierced me like a spear, because I could not share them. Several times I have tried to give love, but either I had lost the knack of it, or the recipients had no use for it as a commodity. More and more I feel that no one wants love. It is too deep. It is given away for nothing but, having accepted it, the payments are endless, the install-ments unending. The hours I had with Helen have been paid for by years of painful memory.

For some men, women are a distraction; love a game, a sport. For those whose love is of the body only, their loves are soon forgotten — they differed so little from each other — are so easily replaced. The belly of one young girl is like the belly of another. They are harder to remember than fox terriers, some of which are interestingly, or curiously, marked. But for me it has not been that way. Women have been my life, my mainspring. The force that drove, sus-tained, and finally destroyed me, because I thought woman was the end and not the beginning. I thought she was the room and not the doorway. I thought she was happiness, instead of the means of achieving it in her company. Happi-ness is something that must be shared. Women are life. One cannot make a sport of life.

We are deceived by the astonishing stupidity of most women. It is only later that we see that there is no need for them to be clever. That perhaps God, having given them so much, decides he has done enough, for certainly the clever women, the career girls, have lost something more valuable than their brains, in the virgin gentleness that belongs to all more simple women — the mother's milk that flows out to the lover as much as to the child. The music of hair and eyes. The cool, soft hands that calm the beast in man. It is her compassion that holds him. Only a woman can put a song in a man's heart, or tears into his eyes; only the love of man, or beast, or the sight of beauty, which are all part of his woman-experience, his woman-self. Only woman can curb his anger, gentling him like a horse, check his cruelty, blunt the sword of his lust without castrating him.

But this is after knowledge. The event is passed. Not only has the horse gone but the stable is destroyed.

I do not know what this beauty is that I have spent my life seeking. Epitomized in woman it remains a mystery, snake-subtle, in so little does beauty, perfection, differ from the ordinary good, the pretty, the near-beautiful that it escapes most people, so ephemeral is this extraordinary quality that it would almost seem that its appreciation is a kind of technique, an art, that only strikes a chord in the trained observer. So fine is it that engineering terms, in thousandths of an inch, in rifle calibres as it were, are required to explain it. The thickness of a woman's stocking or its equivalent, can make the difference between a beautiful and an ordinary leg; a single pound of weight wrongly distributed; the lack of fire, of a burning spirit within. The good and the bad. The black and the white. It is the fineness of the difference that interests me. The perfect fit, as it were, of the cartridge into the breech of its context. In this sense, happiness can be beauty — a radiation of joy, but so, too, can tragedy, even horror. Beauty need not be good any more than power need be.

When I had a garden, each day I would go into it and pick the most beautiful flower for my desk, where I would set it in a fine green Venetian glass vase, shaped like a flask.

The most beautiful rose, the most beautiful iris, the most beautiful long-spurred, bicolored columbine. How did I make my choice? With how little difficulty? Among so many lovely flowers why was one outstanding? All were glorious in the early sunshine, jeweled with prismatic dew. Yet one was always the best. One moved me. So it is with lovely women, the flowers of the city. One is outstanding in a crowded street, one causes the heart to leap, the head to turn. In a line of dancing chorines we say: That one. That one. And the others, all nearly as good, picked like matching horses, fade into insignificance. In horses, cattle, dogs, trees — anything in each sort — there are those which stand out as kings and queens of their species upon which God has seemed to lavish special care, as if, having made a hundred, he had rubbed his eyes and said: "Come, come, this will not do." And has created a masterpiece.

Is this appreciation of God's work a gift of God? Is it a little piece of God within us that recognizes it? Do the Hollywood talent scout, the plant and animal breeder, the artist, the collector and the priest all share a common gift? Are all, each in their own way, inspired? And where does inspiration end and madness begin? At some point the God-inspired love of good, of beauty, merges into the devil's greed, avarice, jealousy and lust for possession. This seems to be the point where I have balanced myself, climbing up one way and then falling down the other, living always midway between inspiration and madness.

One after another they have followed each other, these girls and women. Each one, for her time, the focus of all desire. Each in her time, titillating, tempting, with glimpses of soft palm-filling breasts, each showing her legs, and more leg, till leg becomes soft satin white thigh, lace-edged, demanding. Each, her lacquered fingers outstretched and closing, caressing gently, pulling. Each soft-mouthed, asking. Each so different, yet each so much the same. Each complete in her knowledge of men and their desires. Each aware of her power. Playing each calculated exposure as if it were a move in a game of chess, and knowing that theirs must always be the final, winning move. Theirs the check.

The moves are even stylized — the face turned upwards when helped on with a fur coat, the pull downwards as they lie with one knee raised on the sofa in the half-dark. The quick look, the intimate for you alone, when you come into a room full of people. The look that says: Two hours ago I was naked in your arms, and see me now, so sleek, so calm, so poised. Isn't it fun because only we know about it, only you and I, of all the world? Maybe it would be fun, if most of the other women in the party had not the same thoughts, memories, and hopes. If there had not been men before me, if there would not be others after me. Yet at the moment there is a feeling of elation. The wild smell of her arctic fox as you help her on with it is an aphrodisiac. So is her perfume, the odor of her toiletries, mixed with the subtle emanations of her desire, as wild as the smell of her furs, that rise like an aura from her body. The knowledge of her that is still in your hands and eyes.

Silks, taffetas, furs, satins, laces, perfumes, these are the panoply of love, the caparisons of desire, the sophisticated curtains that divide those who can afford them from those who cannot, and the animals. How odd that man should seek escape into oblivion through such a route. Escape through women, and drink and drugs. But why must he escape? What is he escaping from? His humanity of course. It is very hard to be a man. Here, there is little difference between the rich and the poor. What difference there is, is one of degree. The show girl instead of the waitress, French wines instead of bathtub gin, silk instead of rayon. But the gods must laugh because at the distance from which they view us these differences on which we set such store are invisible. They must think it funny to worry about such things, for there is only the act. There are only male and female. Only principles. Pretty, rich, beautiful, soft, luxurious — they are only little words, meaningless. What is a perfume but a stink which men have been conditioned to like? What is a woman's body but a womb? What is a man's but an instrument for planting seed? A trowel for her body? Wound up like mechanical toys by the forces that drive them, men and women run along the rails of proximity into an embrace which they think they have willed. Both are the victims of life, both the seducer and the seduced.

I shall die without having had children, without issue, as it is termed. I do not count Marie-Thérèse's doubtful bastard. Nor have I ever wanted them. The women by whom I might have had them were not the maternal type, neither by temperament nor configuration. Slim, small-hipped, boyish-looking women have always been my taste. It is interesting to think of the way we condemn other races for polygamy when we white men are seldom monogamous unless forced into it by lack of means. The only difference is that our plurality is a sequence. That the women follow each other instead of joining each other. Less moral in a way, since the old are discarded for the new. Abandoned, or pensioned off like horses turned out to grass, though the fields of alimony are a rich pasture for the lucky ones.

When I die there will be no one to pray for my soul, to offer masses, or burn candles in the Christian manner. No one to sacrifice animals, or men after the fashion of savages. No cocks, or goats will be killed. No slaves will accompany me into the world of ghosts. My children are my books, some of which have already lived longer than the son I might have had after the First World War, had he been killed in the Second. Perhaps it was this experience which deterred me. Perhaps it was the fact that today a man's child is no longer his to mold. The wax of infancy and adolescence is pressed by too many hands, exposed to too many influences — comic strips, films, television, radio — all utterly irrelevant to my world of dreams.

Books and pictures are creations too. Hermaphrodite products in which the creator is both parents, the sire and the dam. They are carried in the womb of his brain and heart and born in protracted parturition. They are a part of himself, offshoots, split off from the parent, like the cuttings of a tree.

Looking back it would seem that nothing in the present world resembles that into which I was born. Manners, morals, means of transport, the value of life and money have all changed, so that a young man of today is more divided from his father and grandfather — I could easily have been the one, and still could be the other — by such vast differences in outlook as to make them literally creatures of a different world without means of communication. So that I, by my own will, have severed an endless reproductive chain and dangle upon it as a final link in a world that grows daily more strange, alien and less beautiful.

I do not think these are sour grapes for except for the interlude with Helen they were never sweet to me. There is nothing new about such thoughts, although I do not think I have ever stated them before. There must be many men of my mind. I do not accept the idea of selfishness, for it is impossible to be selfish about someone who does not exist, and I have known many selfish parents.

Death which till now has been an abstract concept, inapplicable to me personally, now is concrete, separated from me only by days or even hours. Now that my mind is made up I am already dead in principle. I am like one of those termite-eaten beams in Africa that look so solid but are only held together by a skin of paint. That is me. I am only held together by the veneer of habit. Dead, but still going through the motions of life.

It is idle to speculate about the future. That question will soon answer itself. After life, heaven, hell, the possibility of reincarnation, of purgatory, of being an earthbound spirit neither fully alive nor fully dead.

But I go naked, empty-handed, as I came. I can take nothing with me. No one can. So that actually, though I have never thought about it before, in all my life I have really owned nothing. One cannot own things. Either they are destroyed while one lives — worn out, stolen, burned — or one leaves them behind when one dies. On earth they linger, passing from hand to hand. How long they last depends on how valuable they are, on how well they have been made, on the fashion of the moment. Jewels, the most beautiful, indestructible and portable form of wealth, are, in human terms, the longest lived, passing from woman to woman, the outward and visible testament of a wearer's physical attraction. All jewels, from the young girl's engagement ring to the diamond bracelet of the courtesan, carry a sexual implication, and latent in each is the possibility of crime. What stories of lust, passion, of orgy and sudden death many of the older jewels could tell! To what scenes have they not been witness!

Aloneness is what men fear. Most of them would sooner be with their enemies than sit alone. The loneliness of death is its greatest terror. In battle men are less afraid to die. A woman is man's protection against loneliness, the act of love his attempt to lose himself within her. But there are other ways. Men build themselves into little social groups held together by love, by fear, by disciplines and rituals. Each man seeks to bind others to him by anything he finds at hand. A man who has money will have friends. As long as he spends it he will never be alone.

A woman will have friends if she is beautiful as inevitably the honeypot or the carrion heap will have flies. They are nature's tribute to the perfection of such organic matter. But I wonder how gregarious man really is? If these groupings do not really spring from some ancient tribal instinct, if man's fear of being alone is not based on his knowledge that he cannot live alone? Men are like wolves. They must hunt in packs. Like wolves they follow a leader, ever ready to pull him down if he fails or weakens.

Only the artist seems to be out of the pack, to pursue his catlike way alone following the mouse of his inspiration. The artist with his drive to create is inexplicable. Why has he this need to communicate in music, in words, in paint, or stone, something that can only be done this way? His way?

Why is he preoccupied with death, with love, with birth, with beauty in all its aspects? I contemplate death but I step back if a car passes too close to me. If I heard a shot I would fling myself to the ground. Then is it pain I fear? Or is this an alibi for my fear of death? The difficulty about dying is that there is no technique for it, no precedent. It is new each time and to each man. There are no passports for this strange country, no visas, no round trip tickets. No tax that concerns us. No forms to fill in. No bureaucrats to placate.

The Extreme Unction of Roman Catholicism with its historic background and endless reiteration must simplify things for those who believe, but death still remains something no one understands. The irrevocable is always frightening. Even the moment when the boat sails, when the plane is airborne, when one feels: Now we are off. Now there is no going back.

My interest in death is more than academic. I begin to see it as the completion of the circle. Perhaps it is the place where the loneliness ends. Certainly it is the last resort of the lonely, the final acknowledgment that life has failed, and the hope that death may succeed. We think we can capture beauty, especially the beauty of women, and hold it like a warm rabbit in our hands. To capture, to hold, to possess is our aim. But when you own a thing you lose it. You are possessed by it in possessing it. Everything is changed, transmuted by being possessed.

Beauty is terrible. It cannot be owned. It is frightening. The mountains snowcapped. The great buttressed forest trees. Blood. The idea of God. A crested stallion plunging. The crash of the waves in a tempest. The fecund thighs and belly of a woman. The heartbreaking song of the nightingale in the perfumed night. The flight of the hawk. A swallow. A yellow hammer calling from a summer hedge. All are barbed with beauty.

In these last hours incidents come back to me. Terrible and beautiful. Once I heard a calf bellowing. Riding up I found it blind. The vultures had pecked out its eyes and were waiting for it to founder. I shot it. Another time I found a cow down, calving, with her udder eaten out by jackals. I have seen the battle dead dying in their hundreds on shell-ploughed fields. In counterpoint there are the beauties that come to the eyes as jewels might come to the hand, lying there in the palm of the eye, glittering, unbelievable. A small buck standing caught in the early morning light. The perfection of an orchid. The moments when one felt oneself one with all living things, the way one cannot do in a city where only men are alive. A black girl like a bronze, bent, bathing in a pool. A newborn fawn lying wide-eyed in a nest of grass. Flamingos flying in a sunset. And all this when one is alone, looking over one's horse's ears, in a silent world. This is our Africa. The Africa of the lion walking calmly over the veld, of the sunbird balanced on the scarlet aloe, of the dung beetle rolling his ball, of the leaping impala, of the fish eagle high in the trees, his white head and breast incandescent in the sunshine. How wonderful to ride over the veld, the eyes moving as we search the landscape, and the feel of a horse's mouth in our hands as he reaches for his bit.

It is all still there — all my life — though far distant in time and space as I try to pin it down, to relive it for an instant, to say, as it were, goodbye.